SELF-PORTRAIT

WITH WOMAN

The Beautiful Mrs. Seidenman

A Mass for Arras

SELF-PORTRAIT
WITH WOMAN

BY

ANDRZEJ SZCZYPIORSKI

TRANSLATED BY BILL JOHNSTON

GROVE PRESS

NEW YORK

Autoportret z kobietą
First published in Polish by Biblioteka Diogenesa, Poznań
Copyright © 1994 by Andrzej Szczypiorski
All rights reserved, Copyright © 1994 by Diogenes Verlag AG, Zurich
Translation copyright © 1995 by Bill Johnston

Published simultaneously in Canada
Printed in the United States of America
FIRST EDITION

Library of Congress Cataloging-in-Publication Data

Szczypiorski, Andrzej.
    [Autoportret z kobietą. English]
    Self-portrait with woman / by Andrzej Szczypiorski; translated by Bill
Johnston.
        p. cm.
    ISBN 0-8021-1567-5
    I. Johnston, Bill. II. Title.
    PG7178.Z3A9613 1995
    891.8'537—dc20 95-35503

Design by

Grove Press
841 Broadway
New York, NY 10003

10 9 8 7 6 5 4 3 2 1

I

Now he could hear a buzzing on the line. A warm, dirty rain ran down the glass. The air smelled of soot or of some nameless poison.

Tuesday, he thought. It makes no sense that it's Tuesday. But nothing else makes sense either.

He could clearly hear the line buzzing in the receiver. A boy in jeans and a tattered leather jacket stood at the next booth. His white sneakers were soaked, and he was jumping up and down as if he were dancing, with no sense of rhythm, stupidly, mindlessly, as though he were trying to warm his feet. He had red hair, small, slanting, malevolent eyes, and bad teeth. He smelled of mint, chewing gum maybe; he spoke into the telephone in a singsong accent, using the secret language of the obtuse, unwashed chosen ones of fate. He kept saying "like" the whole time, that was pretty much all he said; and Kamil was convinced that she was responding the same way, from the boyfriend's phone he could hear the distant, muffled "like," they communicated this way in the language of cannibals, or long-extinct, fossilized animals, or maybe he was the one who'd lost the power of speech, for these two said the word "like," the keyword, it meant many things in their language, maybe even everything, like they both said, like, let's go, like, Hala, like, Dzidek, like, no, like, yes, like, Hala, like . . .; that was exactly how they spoke, as if they were calling to each other from the chasm of sleep, and Kamil concluded that they were the clever ones, like, they were the clever ones, like, he should die by this pay phone, like, so she had lied after all, like, not an hour ago, using that same tongue of untruth in which she tried to enmesh me, with that tongue of falsehood and betrayal she touched my lips and at that time she already knew the hour of falsehood and betrayal was coming. And what do You have to say about that, God of poets and muleteers, like? Like, Hala, like, Dzidek, like, Jesus Christ, Savior of the sinful, where were You to watch over me, that better thief who was crucified at Your right hand and to whom You promised the kingdom? Like, Hala, like, Dzidek, like, Lord, where are Your trumpets of Jericho, bringing down the walls of servitude and falsehood?

It was drizzling, there was a lot of traffic, the highway was wet, it shone in the silver glare of the headlamps. Big trucks passed by, the rumble of their engines filled the rain-soaked air, and yet it was very quiet, as if the earth had died or had fallen asleep, or had closed its eyes the way old, tired people do when they want to wish others well or to bless them.

The car stood on the hard shoulder; the rain lashed

down, steamed-up windows, dusk, nothing but the head-lamps of the huge transcontinental trucks shimmering in the wet air, a strange smell around, a certain unease in her hands as she suddenly started stroking his face. In the dusk he could see her ash-blond hair brushed back and fastened behind with a barrette. He saw the indistinct features that he knew from his dreams. She was wearing a crimson blouse, jeans, high-heeled shoes; she was tall, slim, she had warm hands, rather full lips, green eyes set in dark lashes.

Yes, thought Kamil, it was right then, in the moving lights of those powerful headlamps, that she kissed me. But when her mouth moved close, I thought she would touch my cheek with her lips. That wasn't what I wanted. I wanted a kiss from her, so I touched her lips with mine. For a moment I thought I was in the world of first experiences, when I didn't yet know the difference between a taste, a scent, and a breath. A very gentle and pure feeling, such as I've not experienced in years, for I'm a sinner and have done many bad things, and I didn't deserve what she was offering me.

He stood motionless, still listening to the noise of the dead telephone line. The dirty kid in jeans had gone back off to his pit. The place stank of disinfectant. The worn floor was covered with shoeprints.

I'm going to die, he said to himself, because I can't live like this. I mean, who would have thought it? Me, about whom it was once said that I have eyes like golden bees, that's what Theophane said, look what's happening now. Have you got the time? Nine. Seven minutes to nine. And where am I? I'm in Warsaw, the capital city, which was once sacked by the devil, but which survived with God's help so as to go on sinning, still dissolute and degenerate, and waiting for the Second Coming.

The ten thousand dollar question: Why did she lie?

Maybe she couldn't help it. Not everyone can live in truth.

He thought about how the women who had brought him up had been different. Fire and water, flood and drought, light and darkness, everything had been given to those women, they had got the best parts. But they were gone.

Maybe she couldn't help it, maybe she had been brought up that way in this kingdom of falsehood, fraud, and dissoluteness, so it wasn't her fault, look around, as far as the eye can see the world is completely flat, Ptolemaic, here no sin can surprise anyone since all sins have become commonplace.

He thought to himself that her men were not to blame either. They couldn't bear any responsibility for the degradation of the whole world that was given to them. Was it their fault that life had not tested them enough?

He thought to himself that these men were better because they were quite simply not so tired, they still had some chance of proving themselves, while his opportunities had all been missed. And what about my freedom, he asked, what about that, Lord? Thou shalt not kick against the pricks, saith the Bible. And I never kicked. But what kind of pricking spear is it, Lord, that You have aimed at my breast? I deserved better. If I'm to be wiped off the face of the earth, then it should be with more pathos. Aren't

You embarrassed, God of concentration camps and gulags, by this pettiness? Where are you this time, Schubert, now that you're really needed? Where have you gone to, Schubert, right at the very moment when we should stand by each other, shoulder to shoulder? And what use are you, Schubert, when at such a crucial moment you desert me?

He stood and stared at the telephone booths, then at the street through the glass, at the rain. Like, like, he thought, like, like, I can't speak their language, it's the language of savages, like, like, where were You, Lord, when she was lying, You'll scream at a person and rail at them to kingdom come when they're about to bear false witness or covet their neighbor's wife, but You won't raise a finger when she betrays a person quite gratuitously. When all's said and done, she really didn't have to do it, she could have told me to go to hell, like no, like I don't feel like it, and several more likes, and in the end I would have got the message. . . . But humans are creatures who are supposed to take responsibility, so if there in the flash of lights on the highway, in the rain and the pounding of the heart, she kissed this poor wretch who had eluded all the tyrants of the age, how was it that an hour later she was able to lie?

He stood alone in the dark, dirty hall with pay phones lining the walls. Someone who had just walked off had forgotten to hang up the receiver, and Kamil heard the insistent buzzing of the phone, quieter, louder, quieter and louder again, because the receiver was dangling loosely on the cord, moving to and fro across the wall, Kamil liked its shadow as it looked like a small, delicate, boyish figure hanging from the gallows.

Like, like, he thought, why did my courage desert me then? But he didn't know when his courage had deserted him, or whether it had happened at all, and he seemed to understand that in his life there had never been a moment like this before, for up till now he had always felt a glimmer of hope within him.

It was cold on the street, a fine, persistent rain was falling, the sidewalks glistened, the traffic moved slowly. Kamil decided that it might be a good idea to get a drink, like no, like maybe it would, like yeah, so he set off toward the square, towards the gigantic candelabras with their blue, cadaverous light, between the cars parked all over, every which way, anywhere, as if contemptuously abandoned forever, in this new Polish shambles, which every day, ever more brutally was forcing out the old Polish shambles, no longer was there a barrel of sauerkraut by the entrance to the poky little grocer's shop, already there were a hundred different brands of toothpaste, two hundred brands of washing powder, three hundred brands of tampons, it was only misfortune that came in just one variety, but they'd announced that that too was soon to change, he walked slowly, past cars parked on the sidewalk, then it got darker, the light of the street lamps was reflected in a puddle, in the gateway of the apartment building there was only a dim lamp, in the stairwell stood a plaster caryatid with its nose broken off, this is it, thought Kamil, this is it, I'll go and see her, I can't bear these lies, things can't be this way, you have to pay for lies, people like me don't forgive other people's lies, especially those of a woman, so I'll go and see her, let her say openly what was on her mind, looking me

straight in the eye, I'm going to see her, fourth floor, the
door on the left, I wonder what her expression will be like
when she sees me on the doorstep, after that telephone call
she can't be expecting me, what a surprise, she'll cry with
hypocritical delight, and it really will be a surprise for her,
but not the kind, not the kind she thinks, all of a sudden he
stopped and listened, someone was coming heavily down
the stairs from the upper floors, it was a man's measured
steps, where's he coming from, thought Kamil, I bet he's
coming from her place, that would explain the telephone,
now he carried on upstairs, but slowly, one step after another, he held the balustrade that had been smoothed by
thousands of hands, it probably remembered the Russian
tsars, the steps from above stopped for a while, then their
steady sound resumed, who is it, wondered Kamil, that
man must have come out of her apartment, suddenly he
saw him on the landing, coming down the stairs was a big,
broad-shouldered black man in a long, stylish overcoat and
a yellow foulard scarf, the scarf hung down all the way to
the ground, the black man passed him, his face was covered
in perspiration, the whites of his eyes gleamed, he had a
penetrating, foreign smell, this is a dream, thought Kamil.
At that moment there was a cry that filled the stairwell and
the whole building, what is it, called Kamil, where did it
come from, at this point a man in a denim jacket, his face
dripping with sweat, out of breath from running, strangely
pale in the glaring light of the street lamp, gave a piercing
shout that a woman had just been hit on the road, she'd
been killed outright, he shouted and ran on, what's going
on, thought Kamil, where's that black guy, he must have

hidden behind the caryatid, but there were no more stairs, he bumped into a passer-by, what are you doing, the other man cried, watch where you're going, a woman got run over a moment ago, do you want to finish up under a bus too, of course I don't, shouted Kamil, but where did the accident happen, you can see for yourself goddammit, said the other man and disappeared, he couldn't see anything, he kept hearing shouting, and he felt pain, something that couldn't really be called pain, but all at once, almost mildly and cheerfully he decided that any bar would do, so he went into the nearest one, which until recently had been called Kruszynka, and was now called The Pub, and where you could get hamburgers, Guinness, gin and tonic, and occasionally, like in the old days, into a fight.

In the bar sat Dr. Skalenko drinking a carrot juice.

"You don't say!" called Dr. Skalenko. "You don't say!"

"I do," replied Kamil, and sat down by the doctor.

"Just today I wrapped up the whole business," said Dr. Skalenko.

"You don't say," said Kamil.

Then they both had a beer. Kamil said:

"I've got an interesting topic for comparative research for you."

"Is that a fact?" exclaimed Dr. Skalenko. "And what would that be?"

"About lying. Lying by age group, according to sex, level of education, and attitude to God. What do you say to that, Doctor?"

Skalenko took a sip of beer. He looked like a wise old

bird, but he gave an evasive answer, that that wasn't a matter for his laboratory, that he didn't deal with such issues.

"Anyway, where did you get the idea from?"

"Brilliant, eh?" said Kamil. "People lie so rarely, don't
you think, Doctor? Where could I have got that idea . . . ?"

"They do lie, they do," agreed Skalenko. "All the
time, everywhere. Poland is no exception. The Americans
once did a study . . ."

"The Americans have done everything," said Kamil.
"But nothing has ever come of it."

"Perhaps it has," said Skalenko.

"I don't think so," said Kamil.

He really enjoyed talking with this guy.

"So I should go? You think I should," he said.

"It'll be an interesting experience. Don't back out
now. Besides, I have your consent, it's too late now to
change your mind, they're very efficient, they've already set
in motion their little machine of preparation, they've
already committed themselves, no, no, you really must
go . . ."

"I will," said Kamil. "So you say that people lie everywhere, eh? I'm really interested in the way women lie to
men. At what moments, and also with what purpose? You
should write a postdoctoral dissertation on that. Is that a
bad topic, Doctor?"

"An excellent topic," replied Skalenko. "Treat the
trip as a holiday, a form of rest, a few days' vacation."

"Naturally," said Kamil. "Because I find it fascinating.
The question of choosing the moment. When does she
begin to lie? Is the cause spontaneous, I'm thinking of the

different types of reaction on the part of the woman. What do you think, you ought to know about these things . . ."

"Yes," said Dr. Skalenko. "They provide extremely decent conditions. I've never been there myself, of course, but our institutes have collaborated for a number of years, I've heard from important people, they really do look after you properly, it's well organized."

"Exactly," said Kamil. "It's not about the lying itself, that's banal, I hope you don't think I'm naive, when it comes down to it there's no truth without lies, that needs to be stressed, yet the problem arises elsewhere, I don't mean to judge things in moral terms, what's important are certain psychological mechanisms."

"Yes," said Dr. Skalenko. "So fly out tomorrow. Or at least let's say in three days. Will you have another beer?"

"Thanks," said Kamil. "It is an idea, don't you think, Doctor? You could administer a questionnaire to a randomly selected group, hm?"

Dr. Skalenko became morose.

"It all comes down to money," he said. "You have no idea how I'm struggling with the budget cuts. They want all kinds of research findings, nothing is enough for them, they're always on my back, but when I go and say that I don't have the money for basic research, they throw up their hands, I hear the old story about how there's a crisis, and that's exactly why I place such importance on collaboration with foreign institutions. I have to give them something in return, hence my proposition to you, but I think . . ."

All of a sudden he broke off, took a sip of beer, and said:

"That I should have lived to drink Guinness in War-saw is a real miracle. Twice in my life I've experienced a miracle. When I was a freshman in college, Stalin died. And now this Guinness."

"I have bad memories of that," said Kamil.

"You're kidding," said Dr. Skalenko. "You weren't ever in their party, how can you have bad memories of it?"

"It's a personal matter," said Kamil. "But I'd like to return to this fascinating question of lying . . ."

"Don't return to it," said Dr. Skalenko. "Returning's a bad idea generally, in this day and age."

Suddenly Kamil found himself alone at the table, for Dr. Skalenko finished off his beer, stood up, smiled guilt-ily, nodded, and left.

Lord, thought Kamil, why did she lie? It can't be, in a world that believes it's entitled to go on existing, that a woman lies without any reason at all, something must have happened, someone must have been to see her, or maybe someone close to her died, in the end everything can be ex-plained in logical terms, but I need a clue, I don't even know what I need, maybe her smile, her touch, or maybe just death, that would really be an amazing story in War-saw, people would tell incredible tales about a guy who died of love, he was alive, living as if nothing were the mat-ter, he was even planning a trip abroad, and then all of a sudden he died in the middle of the street, or in a bar, he knocked over a mug of Guinness, the beer spilt all over the tablecloth, the guy smashed his head against the table, he just had time to cry out that he was dying of love, but no one believed him, even the good-looking blonde sitting at a nearby table gave a derisive laugh, she probably had her own reasons for not believing that a person could die of love, no one believed it in this city, where for years now they had lived exclusively off the bodies of their loved ones, fallen prey to a blind hatred, and only she believed in love, for at Kamil's burial she wept bitterly and called out in deep despair that if she'd been able to foresee such a turn of events, she would certainly have behaved differently, she would never lie again, she called out at the cemetery, as she wept she looked really alluring, she was wearing close-fitting jeans, the crimson blouse with a broad turn-down collar, high, almost knee-length boots, she looked a bit like a beautiful jockey, a bit like a young SS officer, she stood over his grave, slender as a poplar, her ash-blond hair blowing in the wind, maybe it was also despair that blew it about her head, she called out that he had died because of her lies, then Kamil drew close, took her in his arms, and said, but I'm not dead, I'm here with you, let's forget about all that, my darling, that's exactly what he'd say to her, after dying of love, but none of this answered the question of why she had lied in such a stupid and cowardly fashion on the phone.

So I'm leaving after all, he thought hopefully.

That hope was like a shard of glass in his heart: It reflected some of God's light from the heavens, but it also caused him terrible pain.

II

The plainclothes police officer's hair was combed flat and he had a high peasant's forehead, under which there may have been stirring terrible thoughts of revenge for the wrongs of centuries; he had gray eyes the color of water, not the kind that flows in a pure mountain stream, but the water of the Vistula, reeking of carbolic acid, polluted, filthy, and if someone looked closer into the eyes of that police officer he might even have seen dead fish floating on the surface of the irises.

He wore a mustache, since he probably wanted to be a good plainclothes officer, in step with the new times, and mustaches were gradually becoming a sign of a particular allegiance.

The police officer was sitting at an ugly, battered desk on which there were a few papers, a lamp, and two framed photographs. In one of them there was a little girl of perhaps seven wearing a highlander's hat and carrying a highlander's decorated walking stick. In the other a handsome woman with sleepy eyes and a faintly sensuous smile looked straight at the camera as if undecided whether to fall asleep or take off her blouse.

The plainclothes police officer asked:

"So then, what do we have to say to each other, sir."

It was supposed to be a question, but it sounded vague, so Kamil replied:

"So then we don't have anything to say to each other."

The officer leaned back in his chair, put his hands behind his head, intertwined his fingers, narrowed his eyes, and said quietly:

"I hear you're planning to go abroad."

"That's right," said Kamil. "I am."

"Just so," said the officer. "There may be problems with that. I don't wish to interfere with your plans. Completely new times are here, people are free as birds, the whole world is our oyster, the rights of the citizen really are sacred, and it's my job to uphold them; actually, I always did, there were various complaints about that, but I don't feel guilty, wherever you go in the world there's always a police, and the police do what they have to, I didn't make up the rules then or now, I do my job reasonably well, reasonably honestly, everything within reason, so they can come down on me if they like, if it's of any interest to you, I have no personal prejudices against you, but there are some matters I have to clear up, and that's why I'd like to ask you to answer a few questions, because if you refuse, I'll go to the D.A., I'll talk with the D.A. and he in turn will talk with you and ask you politely to stay at home after all, what use is Switzerland to you, all those mountains, snow, watches, cheese with holes, what do you need all that for, that's probably what he'll say to you, so maybe it would be better for you and for me if we talked for a while together. What do you say to that?"

"By all means," said Kamil. "Who's that, if I may ask?"

"My daughter," answered the officer. "Her name's Helusia. My mother was also Helusia, it's in memory of her, because I loved my mother very much. And this beautiful woman is my wife, sir. So, I'm very pleased at your wise decision. Please tell me where you were on Tuesday evening, between seven and nine-thirty to be precise."

"I've already made a statement to your people about that, I already said that at that time I was downtown, I have a witness, Dr. Skalenko was drinking beer with me in The Pub."

"I'd like you to be more specific," said the plain-clothes officer. "Dr. Skalenko is a nice guy, he speaks very highly of you, yet he has clearly stated that he had a beer with you for about twenty minutes after ten o'clock, so perhaps you would like to think again about your reply."

"Sure," said Kamil, "but I find myself in a rather strange situation. This morning I'm woken by an insistent ringing of the doorbell, and when I open the door I find the gentlemen from the police on my doorstep; they put me courteously into a car and drive me to the precinct. Here some other gentlemen have a chat with me, but up until now no one has deigned to explain precisely in what capacity I'm here, whether I've been arrested, if I'm a witness to something, or whether I'm suspected of something and I have to provide an alibi. If I knew a little more of what this is all about I'm sure you'd find my replies more satisfactory."

"Do you smoke?" asked the police officer.

"No," replied Kamil. "That is, yes, but only a pipe and not very often."

"I gave up six months ago. And you know what, it was a mistake. But coming back to the matter at hand, I can tell you I share your objections. This is the cost of the immense changes the nation is going through. Those gentlemen thought that it was sufficient to organize a revolution, to get rid of the communists, and that then everything would go smoothly. It's clear now that's not the case. There are supposedly no communists any more, there's a new government, society seems wondering, expectant, but most important of all, sir, there are certain legal loopholes. The laws we had were terrible, you know that better than I do, in theory it was a people's democracy, but if I felt like locking you up in the cellar of the precinct for three months or more, I didn't meet with any obstacles. Today that's unthinkable. Today we're all standing guard over your rights and mine, we're the apple of the new state's eye. The problem is, the state's kind of uninspired; if I hadn't been so well brought up I'd say the state was a pile of shit, it's unliveable, because there are still no executive laws, no one knows anything, no one knows what we're allowed to say now and what we're still not allowed to say, while it ought to be that everything depends on mutual trust, we should simply work in solidarity, we're children of our beloved Solidarity and that's all we have left. It's because of this that you don't know, and you probably won't find out just yet, exactly what this is about, I can't tell you myself because I'm just a tiny cog in the freshly oiled machine of a democratic police, so I would encourage you after all to let me know what, where, and when on Tuesday evening, and then you'll go off to Switzerland, the air's wonderful there, there are beautiful women, high mountains, peace and quiet, over there in this sort of situation you'd have found out the moment you were taken in that you were suspected of rape and murder, because they wear their hearts on their sleeves, as you might say, while we have to proceed pragmatically, and for precisely that reason I recommend that you remain patient and keep an open mind about my democratic mission."

"Very well," said Kamil. "Very well. Let me cast my mind back."

He looked out of the window, where there extended a dirty, reddish patch of Warsaw sky. Closer by, on the window pane, a fly was perched.

"The elevator," said Kamil. "That I remember."

"What elevator?" asked the plainclothes officer. "You live on the second floor, what do you need an elevator for?"

"True," said Kamil. "So maybe we don't know each other, hm?"

"It'll be better for you if we don't get to," observed the officer rather impatiently. "I don't like clowning around, I have duties to perform, I have to meet people halfway, you might say."

"That's it," said Kamil, "at that time I had gone halfway. I'd got out of the elevator, I hadn't even had time to close the doors, I wasn't alone but with a pretty young woman, do you really not remember that?"

"What on earth are you talking about?" asked the officer in irritation. "It's not me who's supposed to be remembering but you, goddammit. What elevator, buddy? Where is there an elevator in this business?"

"I'm in a bit of a fix," said Kamil. "Because I don't have any witnesses."

"That's right," confirmed the plainclothes officer. "Now, you were saying?"

"Officer," said Kamil. "At that time I was at the post office, where I made an important call."

"Now there's an interesting thing," said the officer, "especially if we consider the fact that you have a telephone at home, and you don't have to go poking around on the street; you can sit in your own armchair and can even call Honduras or Pernambuco. So could you provide a convincing explanation of why the hell you went to the post office, where as we all know half the pay phones don't work and in the hall there are all kinds of muggers, hookers, drug addicts, and immigrants from Russia who may belong to the Mafia?"

"It's very simple," said Kamil. "I'm not alone in the apartment, there's a lady friend whom I've been living with for several years, but recently there have been certain misunderstandings and tensions between us, I hope you'll keep this to yourself, so anyway there are some matters that I prefer not to discuss in the presence of this lady."

"I understand such things perfectly," asserted the officer. "I can now guess that your outing to the telephone at the post office was in connection with a woman."

"That's right."

"What's her name?" asked the officer.

"I don't see any reason to reveal such details to the police."

"In that case I'll put the question differently. Is this woman called Irena Bem?"

"How do you know?" said Kamil.

"We're not obliged to disclose our sources. But I'd like to ask you what you talked about with Ms. Bem and what time that was."

"It was an unpleasant conversation," replied Kamil. "It was around eight o'clock, maybe later."

"Let's backtrack," said the plainclothes officer. "Five in the afternoon, if you please."

"At that time I was out of town."

"Whereabouts out of town?"

"I was driving towards Radom."

"You have a Toyota Corolla, cherry-red if I remember rightly, though I'm a little color-blind," said the officer.

"That's right, a Toyota. What of it?"

"A certain Kazimierz Marcinkowski," continued the officer, and reached for a paper on his desk. "That's it, Marcinkowski. He's the driver of a Volvo truck, those massive big things, you know, they're far from easy to drive, anyway this Marcinkowski says that you were indeed on the highway near the town of Białobrzegi."

"What's this about?" asked Kamil. "What's this about?"

"If it was you in the Toyota Corolla that was parked rather awkwardly on the hard shoulder, so awkwardly that those big transcontinental trucks had to slow down and go through the motions of passing, which irritated some of those drivers, who are tired working people, then I must also assume that when you parked your Toyota on the Radom-Białobrzegi road you were not alone in the car. The police were notified, but when they arrived the car had already gone."

"What's this about?" said Kamil. "I can't stand this."

"What can't you stand?" asked the plainclothes officer. "I ask you some polite questions concerning certain straightforward situations, and all of a sudden you say you can't stand it. That really surprises me. I've been sitting behind this desk for many years, and no one's spoken to me like that before. So who were you with in the car?"

"You know I was with a woman."

"Very good," said the officer. "There's no need to get upset right from the word go. Poland gives the impression of being a big country. But it's really a very small, intimate little country where everyone knows everything about everyone else. I've always believed that lifestyle is a matter of scale. Was it possible here to build a true socialism, like in Russia? It was not possible, sir. When you don't have a Siberia, where are you going to pack off all those troublesome guys to? The farthest you could send them would be Karpacz. Or Suwałki. From there anyone could make it back home on foot in a couple of days. This country was too small for Soviet socialism, and when you live in such a chicken coop you have to make other plans for national salvation. But today it turns out that our Poland is too small even for you, you take a ride to Białobrzegi and the police are informed of it immediately. I don't mean to ask about the topic of the conversation, because that's a personal matter, but I have to know one thing: Did you end up having an argument?"

"Quite the opposite," said Kamil with sudden animation.

"Let's go back to the telephone call," the officer went on. "You say it was eight in the evening. You got back to Warsaw around seven, right?"

"About then."

"And then she went home, yes?"

"Yes."

"There's something I don't get," said the officer. "You left her around seven, even a quarter past."

"Yes. I think so."

"We can assume it was a fairly amicable parting, in any case there was no quarrel, that's how you described it."

"Yes."

"And not an hour has passed before you run over to the post office to call her from a public telephone," said the plainclothes officer. "What for? Had you forgotten something terribly important, something urgent? What was it that you had to tell her immediately only forty-five minutes after leaving her? What was it?"

"You're badgering me."

"I'm badgering you?" shouted the officer. "Listen, I never expected that from you. I'm badgering you? You might expect that from someone inexperienced, a skinhead, one of those hoodlums from the extraparliamentary opposition, who're here for the first time in their lives, but you, who know every waiting room of the Citizens' Militia like the back of your hand, speaking of which, how many times were you in the joint during that recent heroic period of ours, seven or eight, it's hard to keep track, unless it's for posterity and the grandchildren, and you talk so severely about my lawful behavior. It's hard to believe you were talking about badgering!''

"You're badgering me," repeated Kamil.

"Fine," agreed the officer. "So be it. When it boils down to it, both of us, each in his own way, fought for the freedom of our homeland. Very well. Not another word on that subject. It's eight o'clock. The post office. You call her. What then?"

"It was a short conversation," said Kamil. "In substance it was insignificant. I asked how she felt."

"How she felt?"

"That's right."

"And what then?"

"Nothing more. I think that was all."

"And she said she felt okay?" said the officer.

"Something like that," muttered Kamil.

"And that was the end of the conversation?"

"Yes and no," said Kamil. "Yes and no."

"It's all crystal clear," summed up the officer.

"It took some time," Kamil said suddenly, "because after the first conversation I tried to call Ms. Bem again, but the line was engaged."

"And what then?"

"I'm embarrassed to admit it," said Kamil, "but I

called several times, insistently; it's not so easy for a man of my age, at the post office, in the presence of other people, to keep trying like an idiot, every few minutes, it's a very tiring occupation, you're right about the telephones not working, that made things more difficult, I wasn't sure whether she was actually on the phone or whether there was a fault on the line, that gave me a glimmer of hope, but after a while I realized that she simply didn't want to talk to me. She'd taken the phone off the hook. In actual fact she had a reason, because during the first conversation, when I asked her if she was alone, she gave a vague answer that could have been understood in a number of ways, I was in a bad state psychologically, you need to take that into consideration."

"Sir," said the officer, "if I hadn't taken that into consideration you wouldn't be sitting here in this room right now. So that evening someone was with her in her apartment?"

"I can't say anything about that. I still hope that in fact she was alone."

"What time was that?"

"What?"

"Your last attempt to call her?"

"Maybe nine."

"You are a patient one," exclaimed the officer admiringly. "And then what?"

"Then I went out onto the street. Went for a walk. The Pub. There I met Dr. Skalenko."

"That checks out," said the officer. "Did you see the accident with the woman who was hit by a bus?"

"I didn't hear anything about that."

"You must've been there. There was a terrible commotion on the square. It was right when you passed by there. Unless you didn't pass by there."

The plainclothes officer stared at Kamil intently and smiled slightly; the smile revealed his teeth, which were curiously small in that broad peasant's face of his.

"So how was it with the accident?"

"Yes," said Kamil. "Now I remember. There was an accident. I was walking on the roadway. Someone told me not to walk on the roadway."

"What time was that?"

"I don't know; I don't know."

"Yup," said the police officer. "You were lucky."

"I was lucky?"

"Yes. You were damn lucky. There was someone at her place."

"You call that lucky?"

"I do," said the police officer. "Real lucky."

III

"Do you have *Stern?*" asked Kamil.

"The second pocket from the left," said the tall, good-looking blond flight attendant. "Right next to you."

"I'm 6B," said Kamil.

"That's right," confirmed the flight attendant.

He found the copy of *Stern* in the pocket, sat down, fastened his seatbelt, and put on his glasses.

Behind him someone said quietly:

"That Hulse isn't going to react."

A second voice replied:

"Amazing."

"Yeah," continued the first voice. "That Hulse is a waste of time."

I'm at home, thought Kamil to himself, and opened *Stern*. The engines had already been turned on. The plane was taxiing to the runway.

I must be mad, Kamil was thinking, why am I going there? What's the point? What do I hope to achieve? The only consolation is that these dumb crates crash. After all, they're heavier than air, it's only from time to time that they manage to stay up in the sky till the nearest airport.

They took off all the same.

Kamil looked out of the window. Warsaw disappeared at once and that brought him relief, as if something had finally returned to normal. Down below there extended a series of dirty little gray fields and strips of road along which cars were crawling.

I must be mad, thought Kamil, I don't stand a chance, I'll never get away. I left that skeleton in the closet. Even if I get away now they'll catch up with me.

The flight attendant asked if he'd like a beer.

"Yes, please," he answered.

He drank his beer and didn't read *Stern*. Once again he took the letter out of his pocket, and once again he read it through, word by word, carefully, slowly, dully, as if he were chewing over what was to come.

Dear Sir,

I expect Dr. Skalenko has already spoken to you about my idea for a series of documentary interviews with persons from Eastern Europe. I have been at work on this for over a year; the project is commissioned by Radio Geneva. The recordings I am making are intended solely for the archives, and excerpts will be broadcast only in exceptional cases, with the consent of the interviewees. In principle, however, the recordings are not intended for publication but are meant to be used for research purposes. As you are well aware, in the last few years Eastern Europe has undergone huge changes, and the fall of the communist system and the liberation of the peoples of this region have become events of immense historical significance. My proposal to you may seem somewhat surprising. However, such a choice of interviewees is an important feature of the overall research program. Dr. Skalenko is a prominent sociologist and I owe a great deal to his enterprise. My fellow researchers and I came to the conclusion that only a selection based upon a random sample could produce fruitful results. We are not interested in the accounts of public figures, those deeply engaged in political issues or in the struggle on one side or another of the conflict. Such accounts are readily available and may be obtained without any special efforts. And yet, while they are entirely trustworthy, a point which is not in question, they are also tainted both by the nature of the speakers, people accustomed to expressing their views publicly, and by the generalizations which they usually have ready to hand. Public figures, including intellectuals, are not of interest in this archival project. Our guiding principle is to create documentation of the experiences and reflections of those less well known to the public, those who do not play an influential role in society. People like these, who are free from certain obligations to others, are wont to be more spontaneous and open in expressing themselves.

We intend to treat the interviews as unconstrained reminiscences from which may emerge the broader context of the issues and events in which the speakers were involved, not always even fully consciously. For this reason we do not expect our interviewees to make any special preparations; quite the opposite, we want those we invite to tell the story of their own lives in their own way, including those little details that may seem banal and yet are invaluable in conveying the atmosphere of everyday life, mores, and so on. Dr. Skalenko, whom we authorized to identify participants in Poland, singled you out partly because you were once a professional tourist guide in your home city; this allows us to hope that you are a good conversationalist, that you speak fluent German or French, and above all that you are able to talk in an absorbing fashion not only about the sights of Warsaw but also about your own life, which will be the object of interest for us.

My dear sir, without an introductory conversation, which we would like to save till your arrival in Switzerland, it is difficult to fix the exact dates of your stay or the extent of our work together. We endeavor to ensure that our guests have a little free time to themselves, so that they have pleasant memories of their collaboration with us. We undertake to pay for the full cost of your travel and living expenses and a room in a comfortable hotel, and we offer an honorarium of 100 Swiss francs for each hour of actual recording. If you agree to our conditions, you may obtain more details from Dr. Skalenko in Warsaw.

Yours faithfully,
Ruth Gless

Ruth Gless, he thought lazily, I can see her already. I had a physics teacher like that once in my dim and distant past. Tall, skinny, going a little bald, with big, red, rather clumsy hands, and yet she had something charming about her, something winsome, I liked her, I even grasped physics more easily thanks to that strange woman. She died in a street shooting, in '42, I think, because I remember I didn't go to her funeral; it was a scorching summer, at the time I was fishing in the Bug, I caught a catfish, but I was a small boy and I couldn't reel it in, a big strong peasant came along, he said, "Look at that catfish, shit, that kid's a lucky one," he helped me, then he gave me the fish, because those were still the times of decent, honest people who wouldn't wrong those weaker than themselves, of course so long as those people weren't Germans, and of course so long as the weaker ones weren't Jews, and so long as something else that I've forgotten, so he gave me back the catfish, and I said, "Sir, I think we should share it," and we did, and when I got back to Warsaw it was over, the funeral of my teacher, Miss Ruth Gless or whatever her name was, I think she was called Miss Fela.

Ruth Gless, he repeated as he drank his beer, Ruth Gless. Maybe she's different, maybe she's small, plump, a size 5 shoe, munchkin-size, for example, maybe she's a huge, tall woman, a feminist with big breasts, wiry hair, a nose for taking snuff; it would've been better not to have flown to Switzerland, where even the Germans develop complexes because of their natural inclination to messiness and laziness, but maybe this Gless is tall, slim, willowy, elegant, she smells of something enticing, something extraordinary, some sort of Guerlain, for example, or some kind of Salvador Dali, she wears extremely tight skirts which are like a case for her magnificent instrument, her violin, or perhaps her viola, and if she's at all old-fashioned in that Swiss style of theirs, Calvin, Zwingli, what haven't they invented to make the life of a woman more difficult, then that case would contain a zither perhaps, to perform on the zither at a benefit concert to celebrate one's career as a virtuoso, would that not be admirable, a worthy ambition?

Ruth Gless, he repeated with some surprise, and perhaps a little apprehension. I shouldn't think about women like that at my age. I'm almost sixty, I feel old, cheated, and ridiculous. How many times can one repeat the same old trick?

Ruth Gless.

She probably looks like Monika. Reproaches, suspicions, animosity. Even what was beautiful in her became unbearable.

"So you've decided to go after all," Monika had said.

"Yes," he replied.

"When are you coming back?"

"In a week. And if I die, then never."

"You won't die," she said coldly. "People without a heart are probably immortal."

"Why do you say that to me?"

"That's what I think," she said.

"So I have no heart? Who removed it? When?"

He was deeply afraid, because he knew Monika was right. But she said nothing. When he left for the airport she wasn't at home.

IV

The bar smelt of cigar smoke, alcohol, and something else that he couldn't put his finger on.

It's nice here, he was thinking to himself, I expect it's a better place to die than elsewhere, a really quiet tranquil world, sedate, no surprises, everywhere peace and well-behaved people. And most important of all, there's no memory here. For what would they have to remember?

There was a smell of cigar smoke and good food. The waiter appeared abruptly. He was tall, strong, graying, he had a prominent nose and mournful eyes. He asked quietly if everything was in order.

"It certainly is," replied Kamil. The waiter disappeared.

He reminds me of someone, thought Kamil. A sense of aversion and anxiety came over him. He cast his eyes around for the waiter, but he couldn't see him. He'd probably gone behind the bar.

Schubert, is that you?

He felt unease, anxiety, emptiness. He bore within him a barren weight that may have been fear itself or merely the anticipation of fear, or maybe one of those shallow day-dreams of a man more frightened by himself than by the whole of the rest of the world. He bore within him a kind of little animal, warm, vibrant, watchful, restless; it filled his breast, scampering about terrifyingly and painlessly inside him, and he knew already that he had not been able to escape.

Then, for a long time he watched the street below. He could see the passage Malbuisson, an inscription that read *Tissus et rideaux*, and a neon Omega sign. It was rain-ing. The sidewalks were wet, a trolley bus moved along the tramlines. A woman in a long black dress ran lightly across the roadway. Maybe a widow, maybe a joyful lover.

This is a good place to die, he thought, perhaps one of the best.

He had an hour's wait ahead of him. Slowly, obsti-nately, he drank the cold bitter beer. The trolley buses drove through the rain. Without a sound, as if from a dif-ferent world. Neon lights went on in the deserted passage Malbuisson. He could see the flickering pink glow of *Tissus et rideaux* in the delicate haze of dampness as if in a spider's web. The wind tiptoed quickly along the wet sidewalk, ruf-fling the hair of a girl at the trolley bus stop.

He had fifteen minutes to wait. He had a bitter taste in his mouth, but it was only the beer, not the ashes of his world. Gradually he thawed out in the smell of cigars and good food, in that strange, quiet, secure, foreign world without memory or recognition, in that good world free of torment.

At last she came. It was a few minutes after seven, the evening stretched across the city like a lazy black cat.

He thought she looked different than yesterday and the day before. It was a trick of the light, he decided. He suddenly remembered an amusing incident from years ago. A crowded train full of exhausted people, the rhythmic clatter of the wheels over the ties, Kamil squeezed onto a hard bench between a wheezing old man and a sleeping girl. She slept leaning against his shoulder, trustful, warm, unseen. At once he fell asleep like her, touching her delicate, childlike face with his cheek; and then at that miry boundary between sleeping and waking, full of despair and joy, he kissed the girl. He kissed her softly, gently, because he wished her well and may not have desired anything other than that she be close to him, in some sort of communion with him to which he could not give a name. They were traveling through a burned-out Poland, it was the first months of peace, the ruins were still smoldering about them, the dead had not been buried but the living had already regained their belief in immortality. So perhaps he wanted from the girl confirmation that they were both alive, and that they both had a future ahead of them. He kissed her tenderly on the lips, and she slept calmly on, or pretended to, for it lasted quite a while. When dawn broke the girl didn't even look at Kamil. She was plain, skinny, she had a flat forehead, pale, thin lips, and eyes heavy with sleep. At that point he realized that she'd gotten the better part of the deal. He would forever remain her dream.

A trick of the light, he had thought then. And now he thought exactly the same, looking at Mrs. Gless.

She was wearing a dark green two-piece dress with silver buttons. When she came up to the table he stood and moved very close to her. Perhaps too close. And when she offered him her hand, he planted a long kiss on it. Perhaps too long.

Mrs. Gless looked into Kamil's eyes with a touch of irritation, embarrassment, and satisfaction. That was how he took it.

She had tied her magnificent hair in a knot at the back, and she wore a silver barrette decorated with green stones, she may even have experienced some discomfort from this, but she was not prepared at any cost to show the world what was most beautiful in her.

A puritan, thought Kamil.

She was good-looking in that slightly deceptive, fraudulent way that can turn even ugly women into interesting, even alluring creatures. She was good-looking because she was incredibly healthy and hygienic, she probably took two showers a day, had three massages, ate yogurt made from the roots of life-prolonging Tibetan plants, spent fifteen minutes on aerobics, half an hour in the Jacuzzi, three-quarters of an hour doing Swedish gymnastics, and a whole hour listening to Vivaldi on compact disc, which had had a commendable effect on her wrinkles, especially under the eyes.

So then, Mrs. Gless was good-looking, and it occurred to Kamil that he'd never slept with a Calvinist. This thought troubled him no end, for he felt that the world remained unjust despite all the changes that had taken place all around. Why have I never had a Calvinist? Kamil asked someone who was close by. However, it was not God, or even the devil, but Mrs. Gless, who replied in desperation:

"Could you say that again? I didn't catch it."

After all, he was a foreigner and was entitled to express himself ambiguously, even downright mysteriously; to cap it all he was a foreigner from the East, where there dwelt cannibals, saints, and prophets, along with a certain breed of cretins close to Mrs. Gless's heart who for several years now had been running among their friends and acquaintances a charitable program called Springtime for Poland. There had been a time when Kamil himself, driven by a patriotic spirit, had spent several cold, foggy nights hard at work unloading massive transcontinental trucks full of clothes and footwear that had appeared in Warsaw thanks to the initiative of some other equally high-minded Mrs. Gless to enrage the authorities who had imposed martial law and to lend wings to the Solidarity opposition.

"Could you say that again? I didn't catch it," said Mrs. Gless.

"No," said Kamil, "I won't repeat it. It'll remain our secret."

"Oh, yes," she said, for what was she supposed to say?

He was not good to her. When they sat down at the table, he began to stare at her in that special way that is pretty much understood in Warsaw but is quite unacceptable west of the Oder-Neisse line. True, there are also women here who dream of such looks by night, mostly in the summer, in the stifling hours before dawn. In general, however, it's not practiced.

He remained silent and stared at Mrs. Gless, which after a short while became a source of distress for her. And that was just what he wanted.

Mrs. Gless, who had a degree in psychology and the temperament of a journalist, who loved novelty, risk, intellectual puzzles, a temperate person, a Calvinist, an athletic woman, well-off, chic, middle-aged, the wife of a businessman who dealt in groceries, the mother of two good-looking, well-brought-up children of school age, the owner of a coffee-colored BMW with leather upholstery and automatic transmission and of a twelve-room villa set among rolling wooded hills from which there extended a stunning view of the lake, even in rain and mist, Mrs. Gless then, a person of great breeding, who had long known that success is achieved by honest work, punctuality, the right approach to one's duties, and that eternal redemption, if such a thing exists at all, is obtained by improving one's own character, and that it's even all right to sin a little so long as you learn your lesson, Mrs. Gless, then, in the first instance paled somewhat, but a moment later her cheeks turned slightly pink, while her eyelids began to flutter delicately, since Mrs. Gless was probably experiencing a moment of exceptional aversion to life and to herself, for this stranger was suddenly behaving outrageously and at the same time, it might be said, charitably, for when it came down to it she was aware that he was now visualizing her naked breasts, and that was decidedly irksome and embarrassing, and yet, something that she found deplorable, fitted in in some way with her own life and made it possible for her to accept it, at least for the next quarter of an hour, which by the way cannot be explained merely in terms of a lost human soul without adding the necessary and distressing information that she had last showed her naked breasts to the grocery businessman two years ago, for since that time the businessman had had a new lover by the name of Gisela, slender as a hind and as foolish as Mrs. Gless had been twenty years ago, or even more foolish, and for this reason Mrs. Gless hadn't had to or hadn't been able to bare her breasts before the eyes of the businessman, since he had other sights to see, maybe even more enticing, though Mrs. Gless was not at all sure, for after all she was entirely happy with her own breasts, thighs, and belly, where only in one scarcely noticeable place the dark, firm skin was slightly callous as the result of an operation on her appendix. His gaze was roving there right now, still silent and intent, like an astronomer with a new telescope.

Mrs. Gless plucked up her courage and said:

"How was your day?"

"It's not over yet," he replied. "The sun hasn't gone down."

For some unknown reason Mrs. Gless felt a little dizzy. With her cold, elegant, wonderfully slim hand, its wrist as slender as the stalk of an exotic flower of India or of Zanzibar, she touched her cheek, sensing the slightly more rapid rhythm of her Calvinist blood.

Actually I'm being a real boor, Kamil was thinking, but she hasn't deserved any better. While the others were suffering hellishly, she was dreaming of some Don Cossack, because if the women here have dreams at all it'll only be that kind. So some Don Cossack or a black from New Orleans playing the trombone by her bedside. If I were

thirty today, I'd screw her seven times in one night and at
dawn I'd throw her body into the Rhône. But since I'm an
old man, I'll spare her life.

"My dear lady," he said in a conciliatory tone, as if he
had no intention of raping Mrs. Gless, murdering her,
drowning her, or simply burning her body in a kitchen
stove somewhere in the suburbs, "I'm looking to be understood. We have before us several days of reminiscences,
notes, you're even going to record my testimony, for it's
good to have a recording of a madman who's escaped from
so many people carrying spades that in the end he's developed an irresistible urge to bury himself on his own."

"My Lord," said Mrs. Gless, and moistened her beautiful, extremely seductive lips with the tip of her tongue.
"My Lord," she repeated.

That Lord of hers, of course, was nothing but window
dressing, and she had taken His name in vain, for which she
undoubtedly should be punished, and Kamil swore in his
soul that at the appropriate moment Mrs. Gless would not
escape that punishment.

"So I'll be obedient and I'll tell you everything, just
like at confession, about which you have only the vaguest
idea here, since it's an invention of the Papists to which the
Calvinist soul reacts with abhorrence. I freely admit that I
share that abhorrence. That's precisely why I decided to
agree to our conversations, and why I categorically reject
confession before some sky pilot in a black cassock beneath which he conceals the equally black soul of a sinner. I
believe that you'll make an effort to understand my problems, for when I look at you, as beautiful as the Matter-

horn, I think I'm entitled to hope that I'll find understanding for my feelings and my barbaric instincts."

"My Lord," said Mrs. Gless for the third time; she was becoming a little tedious.

She wet her lips on her martini and again passed the tip of her tongue across them.

"I'll tell you something cheerful, which should bring us closer together. I'm painfully forthright. For that reason I can never conceal the thoughts that come to me. This is a matter of great consequence. My dear friend. Twenty years ago I would have seen you in a completely different context. I think I'm entitled to say something intimate about you too. Twenty years ago, then, perhaps five years ago, or maybe even last year, I would have demanded a different setting for our intimate conversations. In a word, the pillow. I simply cannot tolerate what you've done with your hair. That knot, that smooth blackness that is currently at the mercy of the lamplight. There's something of a lost opportunity in it. For any man. Not today, but when we've had a good heart-to-heart, I'll ask you to do your hair differently. That knot is cruel, painful. You're simply torturing that marvelous hair of yours, which I'd like to see on a pillow, next to my poor, exhausted, postcommunist head. Now you say something, just not 'My Lord,' for He won't help you in this matter. From this moment on please rely exclusively on me."

"When?" asked Mrs. Gless suddenly in the calm, balanced tone she used with bank clerks when she was giving them instructions about transferring money into her account.

Kamil tipped his head to one side, surprised. In the

distance he could see the passage Malbuisson illuminated by the neon lights, in front of it an almost completely empty tram was passing, the wind blew down the street from the lake, it was almost eight o'clock, people were beginning their Calvinist evening.

"I'm sorry?" said Kamil.

"When?" repeated Mrs. Gless.

"What do you mean exactly, my dear friend?"

"You mentioned the pillow. So I'm asking, When am I supposed to go to bed with you?"

"Come along now," said Kamil.

He stood up, leaned over the table to Mrs. Gless, took her cold, slender hand, and raised it reverently to his lips. The skin on Mrs. Gless's hand was firm and had a wonderful fragrance.

"My dear friend," he said. "Everything in this conversation was somehow predictable. Except for one thing: that I would fall in love with you."

"And that has happened?" asked Mrs. Gless politely.

It was only now that he noticed she had very beautiful eyes, oriental in shape, in outline resembling dates, or the small sailboats that can still be found on the Sea of Galilee, with yellow or red sails, in that soft wind, in the scent of tamarisk trees, just like in biblical times, or even earlier. Mrs. Gless's eyes were a singular brown color, the whites replete with a very dark, dense radiance, while deeper, in the very soul of her eyes, there glowed the tiny glimmer of a promise.

"I'm not certain, but I'm on the right path," said Kamil.

He found her attractive now, even more than he

would have liked. She was attractive because she was like his women in the old days, sufficiently sure of themselves to be always in control of the situation, something he had rarely encountered later, for appearances to the contrary, despite all the talk, all this alleged freedom and enticing nudity at every step, they no longer had any faith whatsoever in their own strength.

They want something more, he thought, and that's why they end up losing almost everything.

And he also thought that Mrs. Gless had enough to be content with what she possessed. He took fright at that thought, for it disturbed the composure he had so laboriously achieved.

He thought that he was supposed in the end to have found himself in that good place where there is no need to try and a person like himself is beyond any choice.

And now all of a sudden something was up in the air once again.

V

I trust you will forgive me, Mrs. Gless, but I'm going to begin unconventionally; in general, I'm opposed to established patterns. What's more, you yourself have stressed that I should say only what I think, recount the ups and downs of my life spontaneously, without worrying about the chronological sequence. Actually, as far as chronology is concerned I can just about keep to it, but I'm afraid I'm going to be a big disappointment to you in terms of content. I suspect you harbor the illusion that we people of the East are terribly politicized. Since our lives were continuously permeated with politics, in the end we succumbed to its influence and our thinking is impaired, we have a peculiar distortion of the senses, like that old joke about the sergeant in the Polish army who associated everything with a certain erotic part of the female anatomy.

I hope you'll take me as I am, with the whole baggage of my madness, my barbarity, and also that indescribable delicacy that the men around here lost long ago. I wish to emphasize this point since I've decided what I'm going to speak about. I'm going to speak of the women in my life; this is an irrevocable decision, I might call it a kind of categorical imperative, and there's no sense in arguing with me about it. Quite simply, I literally do not have any other interests, maybe it's a sort of sickness, intellectual immaturity, or, if you prefer, intellectual hypersensitivity to that which is truly important in human life. It is as it is and I can't do anything to change it. Throughout my whole life I've thought about only one thing. Woman. I'm in no way an exception, on the contrary, we're all alike; it's just that other men are perhaps more polished, schooled, drilled, spruce, which by the way you find attractive. As for me, I never pretend to be someone I'm not, I always remain myself. I'm capable of telling a stranger on the street that she has beautiful legs; besides, they accept it with forbearance, because I make my declaration and vanish from sight at once, thus displaying my disinterestedness and my aesthetic approach to reality.

In this sense, my participation in your estimable program is a misunderstanding, a dreadful error on the part of Dr. Skalenko, who yielded to the Slavic fondness for easy solutions; I tell you, if I were William Tell I would send myself back to Warsaw on the first plane out. If you don't do this, the consequences cannot be foreseen. I rather suspect that the Swiss radio will not recover from such a disaster for a long time.

Mrs. Gless, I can't talk to you about politics, for in my experience politics has mostly involved killing people, abusing them continuously, and even if they remain alive it is only so that others can deceive them, corrupt them, lie to them, humiliate them, and tread them into the mud to their hearts' content. I understand that from the perspective of the Hôtel des Bergues, where you put me in the golden cage of your absurdity, this may even look enthralling, but it's me who's supposed to be telling you my life, not the other way round.

I repeat, there's still time to back out. Tomorrow at dawn I can pack up my traps and fly back to my beautiful home-land, which is at this very moment wallowing in democracy and choking on a free market economy. I even like it, be-cause the women have grown more beautiful. The men not so much, but what do I care about the men? So call it off now. You'll save Switzerland both its reputation and some money, two things that rarely go together. If on the other hand you decide to accept my conditions after all, please don't expect to be given any quarter. I mean, for the money you're offering me I can only sell myself in small amounts, so let's say that you're leasing me for these few days. If you accept my conditions, then I can begin chronologically. The chronology is important, though sometimes it appears nonsensical.

There's something I must add finally. It happens in life that a person isn't equal to the challenge that fate issues to him, and he seeks some kind of refuge. Maybe from failure, maybe only from pain, disillusionment, or ridicule. This journey that I've undertaken as a result of your efforts and the astounding mistake made by the canton of Geneva is precisely such a refuge for me. From what? My Lord, if I knew I probably wouldn't be looking for a refuge. And now, if you're ready, we'll begin the recording.

I once had a pal that I shouldn't have had, because certain men should simply be avoided. For my needs and ways he was a little too well mannered. Actually, his manners meant nothing, but in those far-off times I was ignorant of such things and I thought my friend was very well bred. He wore a camel's hair coat; in those days millions of people dreamed of having a coat like that, there may even have been people who would have slit their neighbor's throat to get their hands on one.

To tell the truth, this guy I knew didn't deserve any better than that. We both used to go to nightclubs, where I liked to hang out because there were lots of good-looking women there, and some of them had not only their own beds, soft and welcoming, but even their own rooms or apartments, which opened up enticing possibilities for me, since I was limber, slim, handsome, young, and I didn't have a roof over my head. I spent hours on end sitting at the bar on a tall stool. In many clubs I had barmaids I knew. They were gorgeous women, no longer in their first youth, with beautiful, thick hair the color of gold or of ebony, their eyebrows carefully plucked as was the fashion in those days, big, slightly weary eyes, which nevertheless were forever lit with the tiny silver lamp of sex, though today, nostalgic for that world of my youth that has been destroyed forever, I've come to the conclusion that it wasn't a lamp but rather

a silver candelabrum, because for those women sex was
something sacred, their bodies were like altars upon which
youth had to lay sacrifices. They had strangely heavy eyelids that bore a coating of makeup, and I liked to taste that
coating with the tip of my tongue, for when the barmaids
leaned over to me to top up my cocktail, when their heavy
bracelets jangled on their wrists, when my nostrils were
struck with the pleasant fragrance of powdered busts, and
the ladies seemed to be asking with their eyes whether I
might not have a moment, fifteen minutes, half an hour,
right after midnight, because after midnight they had a
break, without a break they wouldn't have been able to
gather their strength to fight the world of alcohol, cigarette
smoke, revolution, secret police, denunciations, torture
chambers, the ruins of Warsaw, their periods, their hus-
bands and lovers shot dead, the world of lost youth, jazz,
impetuous acts of patriotism and equally impetuous acts of
national stupidity; at such moments, when those women
leaned over in my direction, perhaps not at all as flirtatious
as I thought then, perhaps just lonely, eager for a quarter of
an hour of tenderness, not the kind that I wouldn't have
been able to give them anyway, but their own tenderness,
which they wanted to offer to me, in order to recover the
illusion of life, a sense of living on, so when they invited me
with their gaze to come after midnight to the tiny cub-
byhole where there was a German sofa from the occupation
and a bare lightbulb hanging from the ceiling that could
never be turned off because the switch was outside; at such
moments, when I knew that soon would come the quarter
of an hour of sacrifice to the savage gods of that age, for I

still remember, painfully, that at those times I had the feeling of dying, no satisfaction, no emotion, only a dull black pain from everything we were doing together, a black frothing pain from the fact that the two of us had not died when we should have, we'd missed our turn, now we wanted to make up, to catch up with fate, and this woman is right now deceiving herself that she's finally caught up with her fate, thanks to me, because now at last she'll be shot dead on this sofa, three years too late, but better late than never, there were definitely some among them who thought like that, beautiful Jewish women who had survived Auschwitz, attractive camp followers and nurses from the Warsaw uprising, girls from the woods and the dugouts whose bodies bore old scars from bullets, grenade shrapnel, and prison whips, so some of them must have thought just like that, otherwise they wouldn't have uttered certain words, wouldn't have called to me from somewhere far away, from the darkness of their lives, from some tempest of theirs, to make myself heavier, to enter deeper, farther, harder, more painfully, and I think some of them thought then that I was the lid on their casket. And they sighed with relief, giving their last breath. So at such moments, at the bar, when I was making up my mind in the depths of my soul that at midnight I would go where the ebony-haired woman led me, beneath the dusty lightbulb that deceptively resembled the lightbulbs in prison cells, or in interrogation rooms, right then I would move my face close to the face of the barmaid, pass the tip of my tongue across the makeup-covered eyelid of a woman old enough to be my mother—and that was how our act of communication took place.

The man, who was often with me in the nightclubs, objected to my relationships with the barmaids.

What do you need them for, my friend? he would ask when I came back from seeing the women; they're worthless. I wasn't a good man, but I also wasn't as bad as he thought, so I would answer that they were very nice ladies and I was fond of them. But he wouldn't accept that.

I'll tell you something important, he said once; they're not worth a thing, buddy. The lack of proper self-determination is the downfall of all of them.

Of course, at that time he didn't use the term "self-determination." In those days people weren't so pretentious. No one said self-determination, or self-awareness or self-knowledge. People talked in a much simpler way, that a person was unhappy, or drunk, or mad; and everyone understood what it meant.

So this extremely well-mannered guy, who stood me a drink from time to time and sometimes paid for my smoked sausages, steaks, or even chicken viennois, for in those times chicken viennois was all the rage, people longed for some sort of luxury, they wouldn't have anything to do with lard, sausage, even pork knuckle, all of a sudden they became terribly refined, even the wagon drivers who delivered coal to the local apartment buildings that had survived the inferno of the war, even the drivers at that time used to wear long overcoats and hats instead of jackets and caps, and I even knew one of them who owned a leather briefcase where he used to keep his cash, and maybe also the denunciations he used to write, because it transpired later that he had been an informer and had told the secret police about people who complained too loudly about the new conditions. In those times, then, as distant and as melancholy as an Andersen fairy tale, people tried to enter a new kind of existence, they behaved in a truly lordly fashion, even the thief would kiss the hand of the whore, just as the Lord God had instructed the Poles, and it was at that time there was a fashion for chicken, a refined, light, elegant dish worthy of better company.

So this comrade of mine sometimes bought me chicken, but more usually alcohol, which I considered something natural, after all at that time everyone drank a lot, together, in a relaxed way, with a rather boisterous gaiety, perhaps with gallows humor, so I drank with him, and he drank with me, but it was soon to turn out that he was a great sinner who was drowning his sorrows because he was a man with a past, and that means something quite different from what's meant when we talk of a woman with a past. The woman has simply loved many men, for which one goes straight to heaven. Whereas men with a past are sons of the devil, even though they're usually just common or garden murderers, henchmen of Stalin or Hitler.

I still knew nothing of this; the man had even made a certain impression on me. One night he says to me:

I believe I'm right in thinking you had a date today with that black-haired Renata.

I don't know what you mean, Longin, I reply.

He had that strange name, Longin, it's rare in Poland, but guys like him are rare too, and even in the times I'm talking about Longin was something of an exception.

Be careful with Renata, says Longin. I wish you well, that's why I'm warning you now.

I thought he was hinting at some sort of complications of a medical nature, and for a moment I even had an unpleasant sensation of anxiety and reproach towards Renata, in whose good graces I had indeed found myself, but Longin leans over the table to me and says:

Perhaps it would be a good idea if you and I had a talk about this at my place.

What do you mean, at your place? I say. Are you inviting me home? Once again, in my naivete I feel depressed, maybe even disgusted, for I'm suddenly struck by the thought that Longin may have certain tendencies, hence the dislike of barmaids, which he makes no secret of and which until now I've been at a loss to explain. But it's all in my imagination, because Longin says with a smile:

I'm not inviting you home, my friend. Anyway, let's go, you'll see for yourself.

I was not yet twenty years old, I was curious about life, I longed for surprises, mysteries, puzzles about the world; so we stood up from the table, moved towards the exit, I was accompanied by Renata's affectionate but somewhat anxious gaze, she was a woman of thirty-five, of medium height, slim, with black hair and huge, expressive, troubled eyes, it was her eyes that had particularly captivated me, like a dark well they pulled me into the depths of the woman, into her woes, she was very reticent, she spoke little, once she said my name and once she said, It's good that you're here, it's good that you're here, apart from that she never said anything else, but in the well of those huge eyes of hers I heard noisy echoes, she carried something within her, I was too young to understand this, but that night I was to learn her secret, so Longin and I leave, dawn is already breaking, the ruins of the city are smoking with a faint mist, we walk slowly down a ravine formed by the remains of demolished buildings, at the crossroads stands a big, shiny, dark blue Horch automobile, a car that belonged to some German general, maybe even Hitler himself, Longin says we're going to take a ride in this very car, I ask him where he means to go but he says nothing, and I, instead of putting my foot down, instead of declaring that I've decided not to ride with him, I suddenly weaken, because I've realized what's going on, I look at the jagged ruins above which the pink line of dawn extends, as if the gray sky has cracked slightly, as if a crevice has opened up through which the new day is leaking out towards us, for the day is beginning, and I hear from far away, probably from my childhood, a loud crowing of roosters, and then the sound of the first

pigeons waking up, and it's a moment of terrible leave-tak-
ing, because I know now where Longin is taking me, I know
now who Longin is, now we will begin a ghastly dance, my
last morning, that's what I'm thinking, getting into the lim-
ousine, it's common knowledge, maybe not here, in your
country, but where I come from it's common knowledge
that the history of the world is always played out at dawn,
only dawn can bring resolution, whoever survives the dawn
is no longer at risk, death always comes at dawn, it's probably an act of mercy on the part of the Lord God so that
everyone can see the sunrise one last time, or the begin-
nings of the sunrise, because when the car pulls out and
moves slowly down the ravine of ruins the sun has not yet
appeared, the little flames of morning flicker over those
ruins, my last morning, that's what I'm thinking, and it's a
kind of dying, I've experienced so little in life, nothing at
all, a few women, a few lashes, a few hardships, you
couldn't even cobble together an obituary for the newspaper out of such a biography, I had wanted to use my life to
write stories from the thousand and one nights, my God,
my God, I keep repeating to myself in the car, why must
this be the end, Longin is stubbornly silent, he's driving the
car with a gloomy solemnity, we're headed east, where the
sky is brighter and brighter, its pink husk already reflected
in the waters of the Vistula as if, out of nowhere, great
shoals of salmon were swimming past the Warsaw river-
banks, the car clatters over the pontoon bridge, on both
sides I can see the enormous metal humps of the sunken
bridges of my childhood years, but those years are gone,
I've grown old, no more bridges, no more city, no more

people, the new world has arisen from nothingness, from the ashes and the shattered stones of Warsaw, a world still quiet, made of velvet, pink as the sunrise that day, silver from our silence, which however will soon be broken by a man's cry, and it will be my cry, because we're arriving, it's an old apartment building somewhere on the Praga side of the city, at the gateway a barrier is lifted, a dark courtyard, like in the good old days when the children of Jewish tradesmen played here with the children of Polish tradesmen, but no one is alive any more, we cross the empty courtyard shoulder to shoulder like two veterans, like friends, then the stairs, a handsome-looking door into a *Sezession* apartment, it really is an old *Sezession* apartment, the remains of the wallpaper can still be seen on the walls, in the living room there are desks, at one of them, next to the window, a man in army uniform is dozing, but when he wakes up and sees Longin, he disappears at once, closing the door carefully behind him, Longin tells me not to hide anything, for the matter is of national importance, I think you know where you are, this is not the place to mess around, Renata has been under investigation by the authorities for some time because she has some ugly sins on her conscience, so Longin would like to hear something from me about this, he'd be grateful if I could testify as to what Renata has told me about her antigovernment activities, at this point I exclaim that Renata has kept her mouth shut, that she hasn't said a word, that I know nothing about Renata or her past, then Longin strikes me in the face with his open hand so hard that I fly against the wall like a doll, he strikes me a second time, even harder, again with his

open hand, and there's something strange in this, something sham, theatrical, I mean they usually beat people with
their fists, pound them the way corn is threshed with a flail,
they have various implements for this, lashes, crops,
wooden spikes, an SS officer once even beat me with a
spade because he didn't have anything better on hand, and
here all of a sudden I'm getting hit in the face in a sort of
gentlemanly way, with a swinging slap, as if this were a
question of honor, as if it were over a woman and not
about an ordinary case of wrongdoing, I shout despairingly
that I don't know anything about Renata, what do you
want from me, I was with her twice on that threadbare old
sofa, and it's at this moment that everything becomes clear,
because at this point Longin begins to die slowly, it's a fearful agony, in stages, I've never seen dying like it since, he
disintegrates before my very eyes, putrefaction oozes out of
him, he screams as if he were being skinned alive, and I
know everything, maybe almost everything, he's hitting me
harder and harder, and weeping pathetically, the tears are
streaming down his face, I pass my tongue over my swollen
lips, I can taste blood in my mouth, one of my teeth is
loose, I can feel a fragment of it on my tongue, Longin
knocks me to the floor, kicking me furiously and crying his
eyes out, he's shouting that Renata is a whore, she slept
with Germans, Longin has proof of it, she slept with every
German she met, that low-down kike, she turned her own
husband in to the Germans to be executed, that heartless
bitch sold out her own father, Longin is storming around
the room, I'm lying curled up on the floor, my mouth is
bleeding, my whole body aches, but I'm thinking fairly

clearly, I'm concerned about my ribs, I think he might have broken some of them, I'm trying to take a deep breath but I'm afraid to call attention to myself, Longin's now railing at the entire world, he's forgotten about me for a moment, he's crying and shouting pathetically, That Jewish whore goes with anyone, without a second thought, I've told her so many times that she has it coming, that one day she'll go too far, I asked her, I begged her, that whore, give it a rest already, Renia, give it a rest, do I wish you ill, have I ever refused you anything, woman, just listen, you could have a nice quiet life, you just have to say the word, I'll arrange everything just the way you want it, why are you torturing me like this, Renia my darling, don't you even breathe you little shit, or I'll beat you to a pulp, lie still, you brat, do you think a man can bear everything, that he's made of iron, of steel, of concrete, I tell you, a man can put up with a hell of a lot, but there's always something that he can't take, before the war I was sent to prison a hundred times, in those days they used to put communists away at the drop of a hat, I've got the scars from a thousand police batons on my back, and from a hundred thousand Russian whips, and I marched five hundred versts across the Arctic, and I traveled by troop train for ten thousand years before I came back to Poland to consolidate the people's republic, and I can even bear to trample on your stomach, and I can even stand your last cry as they throw you out of an eighth-story window, but you mustn't think that a man can put up with anything, because there are limits, there's a threshold somewhere, and beyond that threshold you can't take one hair of hers, one look of hers, you stupid little shit, do you understand what I'm saying to you, is it getting into that thick head of yours, that there are limits that can't be exceeded, why won't she understand that, does she think that God has allowed her to do anything, that stupid, beautiful woman, you're really not too bright, I said things to you, I virtually asked you not to see her, not to go to that little room, why did you go there, why wouldn't she ever let me go, let me tell you so you'll know in future, because she's a whore, Jewish trash, the manure of history, like you, like all of you here, but things will change, they have to change, I didn't go through so much just so Poland could be governed by whores and thieves, so now watch out, kid, I'm talking to you, I'm going to let you go in a minute, I can even give you something for a cutlet and a glass of vodka, and this evening you'll tell her that if she wants you to stay alive she'll take me in, if not the two of you can take up a collection to buy a casket for you, and either way I'll have a heart-to-heart with her, but I don't want that, I swear to God I don't, so tell her what I said, kid; as he spoke he was crying, and he looked ridiculous in his despair, for at that time I still had no idea that a man could cry out of power-lessness in the face of a woman, though if the truth be told it's only then that it's justified, he wept, and I, with the cru-elty of youth, didn't feel sorry for him, though I should have, even though he'd beaten me up and treated me like a dog. I should have, because a time of despair like that, brought on by a woman, can come to any man, and when it does the earth ceases to have form or sound, there is no shadow or light in the world, only pain is left, but what could I know then of the pain of love unrequited or

spurned, I was a kid, in one way Longin was right to beat
the living daylights out of me; but in the end it didn't last
that long, because when I left, the sun was shining brightly
in a cloudless sky and it was nearly midday.

No, Mrs. Gless, we won't take a break; I understand that
this is a difficult experience for you, but after all I did offer
an alternative solution, now it's too late, so please continue
recording.

Towards evening I was at the bar; I waited a long time for
that beautiful Jewish harlot, she usually showed up for
work around ten. When she saw me she realized instantly
that something had happened, because my face had been
badly smashed up, I had two black eyes, my lips were swollen, and then she made an extremely feminine gesture completely unknown in men, she raised her hand to her mouth
and placed it on her lips as a sign of surprise, sympathy, and
fright. She looked so beautiful to me then, she was fragile
and precious as never before, I decided she was even worth
dying for, the angel of heroism stood by me, probably leaning on the bar with a snow-white wing, because right then I
told Renata that she must leave the city, even before dawn
she should pack her things and make herself scarce, go far
away, because Longin was after her, that bully Longin had
designs on her honor, but she was smart enough to realize
that this time it wasn't about her, she'd known about the
secret police officer's feelings for some time, she'd probably already been through some struggles, evasions, scenes,
so she looked intently into my eyes and said that it was me

who should disappear from view, get out, son, get out while there's still time, she said, I'll be okay with him, I've handled worse, that was what she said, that wise, experienced woman, to whom I owe a great deal, for I took her advice, vanished into the ruinous landscape, and from that day on gave that part of town a wide berth.

And Longin left me alone from then on.

Do you like this happy ending? I can see from your expression that the conclusion is quite inspirational. It's also important that all the pieces of this jigsaw puzzle fit together. The young Pole, put to the test, was equal to the challenge, for his honor prevented him from breaking under the pressure exerted by a communist villain. The young man is prepared to sacrifice himself for a woman, but in the end it won't be necessary since she displays uncommon heroism and she triumphs, salvaging her own honor and something else besides, perhaps not her virtue, for it can't be concealed that this she lost in virtually prehistoric times, but salvaging for example her integrity.

Yes, the word integrity sounds good here, though at bottom it doesn't mean a thing. So now you can turn off the tape recorder, the matter is closed, everyone's happy, let's go for a drink, it's not too late. Unless you'd like to hear a little truth, in which case please wait another moment. So, I came to her that evening before midnight and told her to save me, because I had no intention of sticking my neck out for her whims. I told her firmly what I thought about women like her, who care about no one and yield to their every caprice, after which various people have to bear the consequences of their idiotic behavior. She listened intently to what I had to say; every now and then she raised her hand to her mouth, but somehow I wasn't especially touched by the gesture. When I told her she should do everything that Longin wanted, she burst into tears. I argued more and more forcefully. She walked away. I ran after her to that damned little room, remonstrated with her again, loudly called her the harshest names, and when she said some bitter words to me, I showed her I could be rough. Don't turn off the tape recorder, show a little gravity, life can't be stopped, it flows on, it hollows out its course, and truly, my dear Mrs. Gless, it will go on hollowing out that course.

I doubt whether my efforts at persuasion had a crucial influence on the woman's decision, she'd probably already been coming to terms with her fate for some time, but I know that over the following days Longin was very friendly towards me, and she also smiled to me from time to time. It may have been a somewhat wry smile, or perhaps that was just how she looked then.

In the late fall she died. People close to her said that she had committed suicide one day at dawn, after the first snow had fallen in the night, because she supposedly had some terrible memories associated with snow. But I didn't believe that.

I went to her funeral. Various people came, including some Jews, who in those days still existed in the world. Someone in the cortege said that one of the Jews was her husband, which to me meant that Longin wasn't just a murderer but also a liar, though he cried a great deal at her graveside.

VI

In matters of love it's possible either to remain silent or to speak the truth. But I don't believe that love can withstand falsehood, because that involves counterfeit feelings, it's an attempt to distort reality, a manipulation, whereas in love people should find truth, goodness, and equity.

Life has taught me that the fundamental mysteries of the world can be read in the features of a woman's face. You don't have to love a woman to admire her, but when you admire her it's easy to fall into turmoil.

So what about the first face I loved? That interests you especially, right, Mrs. Gless?

Well now, I'm not at all sure that you need to know about that. Someone using the recording archives in the future will learn about my tastes, and that will be all that remains of me on this earth. A rather absurd and sorry prospect for a man who has in fact lived quite a life.

Very well, if you insist. So what were those features like? She had large blue eyes, like mountain lakes, pure and cold, and above them thick dark eyebrows. A straight nose, rather full lips that were always slightly parted, giving her face an enigmatic expression. You could read into this some kind of passionateness or shamelessness, as if this woman were asking to be kissed, and this meant that she was always surrounded by crowds of men, of whom some wanted quite simply to take her then and there on the nearest sofa, while others only dreamed about her. She was the central character in various made-up stories, for none of these people knew she had chosen me alone long ago, that it was to me alone that she spoke sweet words in the darkness, that I alone knew the real meaning of those ever-parted lips. The fact is they meant very little. I believe she had problems with her sinuses, maybe in that beautiful nose with a profile taken from a Klimt or a Zmurka there was something wrong with the septum, anyway, it meant that her mouth was slightly open, but she disappointed me, she was I think the first mature, experienced woman I ever kissed, and I was convinced that right afterwards one had to die, but I didn't die, and maybe that was why, as she panted in my arms, always hungry somehow, I felt a little uncomfortable, because that woman came to me too easily, I did literally nothing and she was mine.

She wasn't my first woman, before her I'd had a strange mysterious experience which I don't think I'll tell you about, it was at the end of the war, far from Poland, in a time of devastation and suffering that the present-day world has fortunately never experienced.

Then there were a few young girls in postwar Warsaw, they passed like a sigh, a few years later I could no longer recall their faces, or their expressions, or even their kisses, and that is precisely the greatest cruelty of passing time, that it's so easy to forget that which is most important of all, the body of another person.

I think I was kind of in love with that girl of mine from ballads and cameos. But it was something of a boyish love. Greedy and foolish, anxious and with a sense of sin. We called her Theophane, because she was beautiful, majestic, and ultimately as unattainable as a Byzantine empress. But she was also sinful, that can't be denied. I'd even go so far as to say she was the most sinful woman in my entire life. Yet there was nothing strange in this, because at that time she knew infinitely more about love, so she taught me, while I was her rather slow-witted student.

In essence she taught me only one thing: that you don't talk about love or write about it, that love has to be done, and that's all there is to it.

A few years back, long ago, I read in Roger Vailland that love is what happens between two beings who love each other. Vailland was no fool. For only a fool could think, believe, console himself at a time of great doubt that love is for example words about love, that love can be talked away or that it is glances, that it is voices, whispers, cries, light and shade, a candle blown out, a curtain parted, a shadow on the wall.

Theophane was a beautiful woman and so she knew what was what. She taught me with her hair, her teeth, her tongue, her whole body, because she knew that God had given us bodies for the very purpose of loving another person, in this way paying homage to the act of creation.

My Theophane was very beautiful. There haven't been any women like that for years, she belonged to an extinct species, for now women are simply mediocre, and what's worse, they've all come to resemble one another.

As I mentioned, Theophane was hugely popular, she could humiliate men, spurn them and ridicule them, those were times when men allowed women to ridicule them, in those days ridiculing a man was some kind of woman's prerogative, while to today's idiots it seems like a stain on their honor, and as concerns their honor the whole point is that they have none, they can stand up to a woman but when it comes to dealing with the world they're as meek as lambs to the slaughter, so she was also able to beat men about the head with her shoe when she'd had too much to drink.

And sometimes she did drink too much.

And at those times, she really was capable of taking a shoe off her magnificent, slim, exquisite foot and smacking the heel into the face of some moron who for a moment had imagined that it was for him those eternally parted lips were waiting.

She was beautiful, experienced, capricious, stylish, and had nothing better to do than to fall in love with a man who didn't know the first thing about love, or about women in love.

I was that man, Mrs. Gless.

I didn't realize that she loved me, at first I, like so many of the men around her, thought she was just a very passionate woman.

I had a pal who fell in love with her; he stole for her, cheated for her, lied for her, he might even have been capable of killing for her, but she refused to have him near her. He annoyed her, she often reproached me for spending so much time with him, it even led to an argument a number of times, because then, young idiot that I was, I thought friendship between men had equal rights with love of a woman, which is of course an illusion of immature minds.

As far as I can remember, that friend of mine was neither good-looking nor personable. Rather rough-hewn, with a broad neck upon which was set a round, already balding head, a peasant's shapeless face without a sign of the thought that turns us into interesting people. He was every inch the bumpkin; yet he had a lyrical soul.

I was his antithesis. I was slim as a young pine tree on a sand dune, dark as a Jewish alley in old Warsaw. I'd seen myself in the eyes of various women, they liked to look at me, almost all of them liked that a lot, from the young girls to the ladies who, with all due respect, had been around the block.

So I was rather handsome in those days, but I was also terribly loyal to my friend, that rough-hewn hayseed from out of town who wrote lyric poetry and wished to slay dragons for the beautiful woman with the ever-parted lips. One day she said to me, somewhat irritated because a few days before I'd stood her up at our regular meeting place, that she absolutely demanded that that evening I come to the home of her friend, a woman called Katarzyna.

Katarzyna was stunningly beautiful; she was known as the Abyssinian, because her face was exotic, swarthy, narrow like the face of a young kitten, her legs were incredibly long, and her hands and feet incredibly shapely; next to her, even my capricious beauty seemed commonplace. The Abyssinian was virtually a legend; she was perhaps twenty-six or twenty-seven, and she had an apartment on the first floor of a villa left standing after the war, and a four-year-old son said to be the product of a gang rape by SS officers after the failure of the uprising.

I think that in my own way I loved the Abyssinian too, with a bizarre love made up of pride and vanity. It was true that once or twice she'd let me kiss her, probably out of absent-mindedness or laziness, because she was sick of fending me off. Besides, she liked me; she knew about her friend's romance so she was nice to me in order not to hurt her. But it would never have occurred to her to treat a kid like me seriously.

I considered myself the happiest man alive when once or twice it happened that the two of them accompanied me into the café on Marszałkowska Street, in the sea of Warsaw's ruins, in the powerful glare of a Sunday afternoon, they walked into the noisy café, where you could get real coffee in real cups and superb cakes about which legends were told in the starving Paris of those times, and I strode between them, a slim youngster, virtually a boy, a pale, intense face, at that time it was probably distorted with a grimace of pain such as can be produced only by a man's pride, I mean the pain of the ecstasy of power, absolute possession, Hitler might well have felt it as he issued orders to immense armies on all the European fronts, but Hitler commanded only men, so he was just a little squirt, a beggar, because I had at my side the two most magnificent women in the city, one as swarthy as a Tartar slave, the other a beautiful, majestic empress of Byzantium. One of the Abyssinian's admirers, when he'd had a few, used to say that in love that woman was like a flute, like Mozart, *Eine Kleine Nachtmusik,* while another used to say, and I think he was right, that when he kissed her he felt something metaphysical, as if the curtain separating him from eternity had been raised.

The other was the empress Theophane, also uncommonly beautiful, with eyes like the lakes of Lithuania, or of the Alps, or the Andes, or of the moon.

And at that moment no one would be drinking coffee, not even the newcomers from Prague or Paris, not even the American spies or the Soviet thugs, if they were in the café. I had no idea how much I was risking with my boundless vanity. In those days men were prepared to shoot someone in broad daylight on a busy street because of a woman, and both of them were worth shooting someone for, not just in the ruins of Warsaw but on the Champs Élysées or in Manhattan too.

At that time we were all like hungry greyhounds, we moved along the streets of Warsaw soundlessly, slender, agile, limber, strong, silent, accustomed to life in the ruins, like homeless dogs. We would sit in those ruins by night in the summer and fall, and even when snow fell from a leaden sky. We would sit in the ruins, the wild dogs of war, young Polish wolves, cheated by life, victims of ill-treatment, lies and deception, for we had been told for years that Poland is important, that the war is important, freedom is important, dignity is important, we pored over Conrad and Żeromksi, Mickiewicz and Słowacki, we fought on the last redoubts, to the last bullet, we died without a murmur, the wild dogs of that Poland, the pups of that world, lied to till the last minute, for no one told us we were participating in a fiction and an absurdity, no one told us that our lives, given to Poland, sold out to freedom, thrown away on the garbage heap of honor, were simply a sham, because that's not what life is all about, but about woman.

And it was only in the ruins that we found out the truth about the world.

One day Theophane told me to go to the Abyssinian's that evening, at sundown. It was a scorching day in early summer; a cherry-red dusk was falling, in the dust from crushed bricks, in the clatter of the dilapidated Soviet trucks, in the shouts of children jumping about in the ruins. From the burned-out ghetto there still came a stench, even though a couple of years had passed, and no one remembered the Jews any more; they'd even forgotten about themselves fairly readily.

A pure coincidence brought about that terrible night. On my way to the Abyssinian's, on the heaps of rubble that separated downtown from the better-preserved northern areas of Warsaw, I ran into my friend with the peasant's face and the lyrical soul. There occurred to me a sinister idea, which I decided nevertheless to put into action at once. I'd been dreaming about the Abyssinian for a week or two; the peasant poet was lovesick for Theophane.

What are the limits of a man's villainy? I've been asking myself that question for years, but so far I haven't found the answer.

That evening the ladies had two bottles of Caucasus wine at home, a great delicacy. In those days people usually drank

moonshine distilled by wily, money-grubbing farmers.
Next to that, the Russian wine had the fragrance of the
Tuileries Gardens before the revolution. When we arrived,
Theophane threw her arms around me in a gesture of devotion and love, but, in accordance with my diabolical plan, I
treated her somewhat coolly. I sat on a narrow sofa right
next to the Abyssinian, while my friend sat by Theophane.

She wasn't exactly pleased with this. But she displayed a
certain obedience in the face of my whims; there are
women who believe, wrongly as it happens, that giving in to
the man they love makes him more inclined to love them.

And then she committed a grave mistake that arose from
my own baseness: She went with the other guy, confident
that by doing so she would win my devotion. The Abyssinian, rather disdainfully and not without a sense of
humor, yielded to my blandishments.

Those were strange times, Mrs. Gless. Women didn't save
themselves for the future, because no one had sufficient
strength or hope to believe in any kind of future. The
whole future was the world that surrounded us then. We
knew by then that things would never be different, never be
better, never be closer to redemption. We'd been given
what we were given and there would be nothing more.
Ever.

So those women didn't anticipate a better future because
what was taking place then outside the windows was the
only better future a person could count on.

At dawn everything came to an end. The pathetic story of a young idiot and a very beautiful, high-minded woman. Theophane bid me farewell with a strange look in which there was pain, but also a hint of contempt, repugnance, maybe even hatred.

When she died many years later, she left behind two grown sons and a loving husband. I heard that she remained beautiful till the very end. And I hope that soon after that night she forgot I ever existed.

And the beautiful Abyssinian threw me out early in the morning, just as I deserved.

The next day I beat my friend to a pulp on the piles of Warsaw rubble. He wasn't mistaken as he cried out to me in despair throughout the beating that I had wanted it myself, that he hadn't done anything against my wishes.

Today I know he was even more stupid than I was.

For a few days I licked my wounds from the fight. Eventually I forgot all about it, because life had to go on. You had to worry about a bite to eat, a roof over your head, a cup of hot water.

Such were the times, Mrs. Gless: too cramped for a great love.

VII

"I had no idea that world was so terrible," said Ruth Gless. "Please don't be angry, but I feel a little hurt."

"Hurt?" said Kamil in amazement. "Can you react like that to the lives of millions of people? By taking offense at them?"

"I don't mean the lives of millions," said Ruth Gless, "but your account. This story is becoming difficult to endure."

"I'm very sorry," he replied. "I did warn you."

"What did you warn me about?" asked Ruth Gless. "No mention was made of your cynicism."

She stood up from the bench and took a few steps in the direction of the quay. Kamil followed her unhurriedly. Yachts moved in stately fashion in the faint breeze that rippled the surface of the water. Bright silver flakes of light danced on their sides. Ruth Gless stopped; now she looked at Kamil with a certain mistrust, maybe with aversion even, but in her beautiful elongated eyes there was a flicker of compassion. She stood still, leaning on the concrete balustrade that separated the broad sidewalk of the boulevard from the entrance to the pier. The glittering, shimmering flakes of light were reflected in her face just as on the sides of the yachts. She's beautiful, thought Kamil with a touch of anxiety, desire, and anger; she's grown much more beautiful these last few days. Have I gone mad, that I want to sleep with this woman? Hasn't there already been enough disappointment, torment, and foolishness? What am I looking for in this city, what do I want generally in this world that has shattered me so badly that for years there's been nothing to put back together again? And why is it still going on, my good Lord?

There was unbroken traffic along the quai du Mont-Blanc. On the opposite shore a massive fountain flung a column of several tons of water up in the air, some rock-and-roll idol blared out from the speakers of a pleasure boat, the flags of the luxury hotels fluttered in the wind, the first neon signs of the banks and insurance companies came on, a silver Boeing like the kind of pike you can still sometimes catch in the Mazurian lakes was coming in to land at Cointrin, leaving behind it a trail like the loosely braided hair of an old gray witch, Ruth Gless's eyes watched Kamil from a short distance, they held a hint of repugnance but also a little charity and hope, sorrow stood between these two people on the smooth gray sidewalk, someone somewhere gave a ringing cry, maybe for help, maybe just telling off a naughty child, Kamil suddenly sighed, turned around, and returned wearily to the bench.

Now they were far from each other. They were silent.

Ruth Gless once again looked at the lake, the yachts, and the fountain. The cars droned monotonously, the sky slowly turned dark and lost its blue glow, and the silver flakes of light faded from the sides of the yachts.

After a while Ruth Gless returned to the bench.

"It's all too sad," she said. "I can't reconcile myself to such a sad world."

"You don't have to reconcile yourself," he said mildly. "You should thank God for your world. I mean it's beautiful, isn't it?"

"I don't know," she replied. "I always thought so. Now I'm not sure any more."

"I wouldn't like to disenchant you," said Kamil. "This trip came at a bad time in my life. I feel a bit better here. For that reason I owe you a debt of gratitude, Mrs. Gless."

"My Lord," she said, but this time that Lord of hers must have been close, because His name sounded like a groan or a challenge.

Kamil said quietly:

"I haven't behaved as I should towards you, I've been tactless on a number of occasions, that is unforgivable, but during our conversations I find in you something very noble, something gentle, something that right now I need, Mrs. Gless, and for that reason I'll put the matter plainly. I'm a fairly shy person, life has never pampered me, it's been a hard world, there've always been too many demands and too little tenderness. No, please, don't turn on the tape recorder, this is a conversation just between the two of us, let's not bother with any of that nonsense, today I'd like to hear your normal voice, just as you hear my normal voice.

I'm not that hard, and my world was hard as can be, that's why my soul has been painfully battered. Sometimes I can be really offhand, but it's not from disrespect, quite the opposite, I'm simply apprehensive. Mrs. Gless, I don't want to talk about certain matters in my life, but I ask you for forbearance."

"What is it you're afraid of?" asked Ruth Gless. "And what are you running away from?"

"I don't know," said Kamil. "I think that like everyone, I'm partly frightened of myself, perhaps I'm frightened of hatred, contempt, humiliation, but most of all, and this is strange, I'm most frightened of love. You understand, things have been terrible in my life, I didn't know how to suffer, I didn't know how to withstand suffering, and what use is the greatest wisdom if a person can't do the thing he was created to do. Just think, what kind of life have I had, when even as a child I was terrified of pain, I believed it was better to die than to put up with pain, and then, as the years went by, I became more and more convinced that that childish belief was right, and I kept repeating to myself that life is worthless when it's filled with a ceaseless pain that you can't name or define, because it accompanies every thought, it is quite simply life itself. I couldn't accept that, and yet that's the most important thing a person has to do. You have to know how to suffer, Mrs. Gless, to learn suffering, to perfect it in yourself, you simply have to know what the suffering is for, because it must be the presence of God in a person, His voice, His look, His sign, and that's why I think that death is the end of our suffering, an act of divine mercy, God has had enough of our torments, even

He can't stand them any longer and so He sends us the salvation of death."

"Why do you think so?" Ruth Gless asked very quietly. "No one should think like that. Even you haven't suffered so much as to be entitled to think like that."

"I'm a Christian, Mrs. Gless," he said solemnly. "There is no Christ without suffering."

"And love?"

"Yes, love too. Because love is an attempt at dying. In that attempt people are trying to triumph over death. But they can never succeed."

"Have you ever said that before to a woman?"

"I've said it to every one."

"Polish women must be strange if they've loved you in spite of that."

"If they loved me," said Kamil, "it was probably just because of that."

Suddenly, almost despite himself, he put his hand on Ruth's hand. She removed hers.

"What are you afraid of?" he asked. "I'm a wanderer from the untamed fields of Europe, tomorrow I'll be gone, you'll forget I ever existed. What are you afraid of?"

"I'm not afraid," she said, and put her hand on his.

"You're very beautiful," said Kamil with an effort, because he didn't want to say it and could feel himself growing rebellious at his own weakness.

"I'm not beautiful," she retorted. "I'm just uncomplicated. That sometimes produces the same effect."

"You're very beautiful," he repeated, almost testily.

He lifted Ruth's hand to his lips and kissed it. She seemed a little embarrassed. He said:

"In Poland that doesn't mean a lot."

"Yes, I know," said Ruth Gless. "These are your chivalrous ways."

"But I have other ways," he said. "With me it means a great deal."

He felt a lump in his throat, he heard the beating of his heart. Why, he said to himself almost in pain, why are you doing this? It's not her. It's not about her. So why are you doing it?

Ruth Gless looked him right in the eye. A warm, gentle wind passed over the lake, rippling the surface of the water, the waves splashed against the sides of the yachts, the cars on the roadway were turning their headlamps on, the huge cherry-red sun was sinking slowly towards the foaming current of the Rhône, the sky seemed oddly discolored, Ruth Gless stared obstinately into Kamil's eyes, he saw the face of this woman in the glow of the setting sun as if it were bathed in flames, a face on fire, fire that he knew so well and she didn't know at all, he was suddenly seized by a shudder of concern, an indescribable anxiety for the fate of this woman, may she be spared, he thought, he didn't know what from, but he felt fear, torment, and also something amazing that he hadn't experienced in years, he was filled with compassion, a sense of tenderness and devotion, may she be spared, that's all I ask, and if necessary I'll bear the burden myself, I can bear anything, but let her be spared, he was thinking this, and she was still staring into his eyes, which she could no longer see clearly since dusk was falling, but all of a sudden, in the light of the headlamps of the cars and the glow of the sun, as red and terrible as if it had been setting over Warsaw, she noticed something in Kamil's eyes, though she couldn't know that it was probably tears.

"Mrs. Gless," said Kamil. "Please pay no attention to what I'm saying."

"When?" she said, completely soberly. "Now, or during our recordings?"

"That was the wrong choice," he said. And once again he lifted her hand, and delicately kissed her palm; he felt some opposition, kissed it again, and then, gently overcoming an equally gentle resistance, touched his own face with Ruth's hand.

"Don't let me do this," he said.

"Why not? Of course it means something, but I'll be the one to decide what."

"When will you decide?" he said quietly.

Once again he felt the violent pounding of his heart. Gently, delicately, with a tenderness that almost hurt him, because he had suddenly felt himself unworthy of all this, Ruth stroked his face. She had frail, delicate, girlish fingers. I won't love her, he thought, I don't want to. I should leave tomorrow.

"Ruth," he said. "This isn't good."

She laughed quietly, and shook her head.

"Nothing's happened yet. Nothing good and nothing bad," she said.

My God, he thought, how little she knows, since she says that. These people here are deaf and blind to certain things. I don't know what it is they don't see and don't hear, but that's what it boils down to, and that's why they live in a world of illusions. This woman says that nothing's happening, yet for the last few minutes on her earth and mine rivers are flowing to their source, wolves fleeing from lambs, floods and fires raging. Doesn't she hear that?

"Ruth," he said. "Our earth is trembling."

Something touched her in his words, because she moved her head a little closer to his to look into his eyes in the gathering dusk. But it was too dark in that place, right next to the yachts, with the bright lights of the cars behind them. Just at that moment the street lamps went on all along the boulevards, a blue light streamed down onto the land and the water, it became much brighter, the faint breeze creaked in the mastheads, the waters of the lake washed against the sides of the yachts and the buoys and lapped quietly at the concrete embankment, an Indochinese boy came past on a skateboard, a man selling waffles called out in a singsong voice to the few passers-by, in the blue light of the street lamps Ruth's face looked even more beautiful to Kamil, intense and filled with a mysterious, feline pensiveness, he repeated:

"Our earth is trembling."

"Very well then," said Ruth Gless in an extremely calm voice. "Sooner or later something has to happen to a person."

VIII

The water in the swimming pool was curiously divided into colors, a patch of green framed by dark blue and silver strips. Ruth Gless was sitting at the side of the pool, her feet in the water; her handsome silhouette in a wine-red swimsuit stood out against the background of the nearby shrubs. Around her head there was a dark, alluring halo. It was her magnificent hair, still wet from the swim, smooth and glistening.

I've seen this before, thought Kamil, I remember her from a dream. Then, on the highway, in the glare of head-lamps, trucks were passing, rumbling across the concrete, one after another, the drivers had tired eyes, everywhere flashes of light, mist and rain, at that time she kissed me treacherously, or maybe it was even earlier, a long long time ago, I remember the dark colors of the water, and a woman's hair streaming in the darkness.

The large white house was all lit up; some of the company had gathered on the terrace. From there Kamil could hear the voice of the man of the house. Gless was pronouncing his words clearly, he was probably saying something about the grocery business, as that was all he ever talked about; by his side stood Gisela, good-looking, slim and frail in the sharp blueish light of the lamps, the kind that are usually used in the morgue during an autopsy.

Sitting in a wicker beach chair, Kamil was smoking a pipe. At arm's length, on a small table stood a glass of Campari. If he had felt like raising himself up to look down between the slender, silvery plane trees, he would have seen a gentle wooded hillside, and a little farther, where in the depths of the night there glittered little beads of cream-colored lights, the shore of the lake, from which a mild wind was now blowing.

You'd think everything was just as it should be, thought Kamil, and yet I feel like howling. I wonder how they'd react. If I got up now, bared my aging fangs, and roared in torment, out of fear of death and an even greater fear of life, if I were to decide to yell out all those years of silence, muteness, and secrets, if I stood up now and began howling; what would they do? Some of them would get quite a shock. Some of them would be made to think. Because it's not so easy, even in this company, devoid of memory and of history, to remain silent in the face of a terrible cry of despair.

No, that wouldn't be possible, even here.

To be fair, they have their cries too. Is Gless in a better position than I am? He turned out to be far from stupid, he realized at once that Ruth had gone to bed with me. After all, it was the first time in months that he'd heard her laugh-

ter in that house. And that young girl who's giving him a
modicum of illusion, a little of that youth that aging men
wish for yet which is always a lie, is she not a sort of torment to him? Gless, listen to me, buddy. Maybe I'll come
up there onto the terrace, among those yes-men in their
dark suits and the babes in low-cut dresses, maybe I'll come
up there and the two of us will have a good, wild, terrible
howl. What do you reckon, Gless, is that not the only
course of action still open to us?

"Don't think about it," said Ruth Gless. "Don't reproach yourself at all. Nothing's actually happening. I'm
lying a little, just a little. You don't even have to do that. So
don't reproach yourself."

She kicked her feet in the dark water, silver drops
splashed up and fell. She stood up. She was tall and slim,
forty-two, health, composure, moderation, and restraint.
And she was far from stupid. She's simply a good person,
thought Kamil, and she knows I'm not telling her the truth,
because in our conversations I pass over what's most important. If she were to hear the whole truth . . . Almighty
God, who in all the world could bear the whole truth about
me?

"Don't worry," repeated Ruth Gless, moving up to
him in the mellow darkness, "I know you're not telling me
the truth."

"Witch," said Kamil. "They should burn you at the
stake."

"They will," said Ruth. "Sooner or later everything
will come out, and then they'll have no mercy for me."

Now she was standing close to him, the wet swimsuit

clinging to her body. Kamil sat up and put his cheek against Ruth's cold thigh. She placed her hand on his head, buried her long thin fingers in his hair. She said quietly:

"Don't be afraid. Nothing can happen."

He kissed her thigh, grateful and strangely radiant inside as if he were soon to die and be redeemed.

"Ruth," he said. "I don't love you. But I'd like to. If I still have some time, a year or two, I'd like to be with a woman like you."

"Nonsense," she retorted. "It's not me. The other woman is different."

"What's she like?" he asked. "What's the other woman like? Does she exist anywhere?"

He put his hand on Ruth's thigh a little above the knee; he felt the coldness of her skin, but he also felt the woman's inner warmth, and that was exactly what he needed.

"You know what she's like. Oh, if you want I'll come to you again. My Lord, do I have anything better to do in this world? But when I come we won't be alone."

"We won't be alone," said Kamil. "Why has God punished me?"

"How do you know it's God . . . was it always God who chose your women?"

She laughed. Someone on the terrace called to them. Ruth took a step back and Kamil's hand dropped.

"I'd rather not have any displays," she said. "He knows anyway, but does everyone have to find out at once?"

"No," said Kamil.

In the darkness he could see her eyes shining. He said:

"Any man in the world would be happy if others suspected him of being with you."

"God," she said. "At last you're remembering your manners."

She suddenly came close again. The circle of lights that fell on the lawn around the terrace gave them cover at the edge of the darkness. She took Kamil's head in her strong, fine, delicate hands and said quietly:

"Tell me now, what's she like?"

"She doesn't exist," he answered.

"Yes she does," said Ruth Gless. "I'll describe her to you. From what you've already told me about yourself I know what she's like. Of course, you believe that you're going to die. You know what, you're absolutely right. You will die. But there's no need to be in such a hurry, my dear. There are still so many women in the world. Let me tell you something. I once had a wonderful man; he was forty years older than me. In those days I belonged to that ridiculous and dangerous category of women that not even you have come across. Dissolute and superstitious at the same time. I wanted to sleep with every man I met, and I was terrified of every one of them. It was even a kind of turn-on. Gless had just married me, he was a nice boy and didn't have a clue about anything. Today he understands a lot more. When I met that other man, right away I knew clearly that he would create me. Like the Lord God. Do you believe in God?"

"Go on," answered Kamil. "Perhaps I'll finally learn something."

She laughed quietly. She shook her head, and her hair,

already slightly dried by the wind, suddenly became a black, disquieting cloud.

"I loved him," Ruth said softly. "He was stronger than anyone. He was the strongest man who ever lived. Sometimes it occurs to me that maybe he was God Himself. At least for me. I mean, things like that do happen, don't you think . . . ? But even if he was God, he also had a certain weakness. Because there came a day when he was dying. By then he was old and sick, for years I'd been doing nothing but nursing him, straightening his pillow, holding his hand when he was afraid of the painful injections. He was weak and ill, but he remained beautiful to the end. I cared nothing for what people thought, or what Gless thought; actually, he was forbearing, it has to be admitted, because he simply understood that the other man was more important to me. Almost every day, every moment I passed at the side of the man who had spent ten years making a woman of me, and then for the next ten years had been sapping my strength and making me suffer. I loved him. And he was worthy of it. And guess what he said to me a quarter of an hour before he died, as I was mopping his face and his brow. Guess what he said then, that man of my life, who had created me like the Lord God. He said then: 'Ruth, I loved you very much and you are a magnificent woman. But you aren't that other woman.' 'Who am I not?' I asked, horrified and hurt as never before. 'You're not the next woman, whom I'll no longer have time to love. I'll never have that woman,' he said. Those were virtually his last words. In that you're like him."

"Even witches are wrong sometimes," said Kamil with

relief, for once again he felt a little derisive. "Your friend could afford such words. He was probably an aristocrat. I'm a beggar, I wander around the world with my bell asking for alms and pity. Never in my life have I taken a woman. I've always asked politely beforehand if I may."

"Yes." Ruth Gless looked towards the terrace. "I think we should be getting back to them. I'll need to change."

A stronger wind blew now from the lake. Somewhere down below a siren sounded. It was a ship leaving the harbor. Kamil got up. Ruth was tall, but he stood almost a head taller than her.

"You're so big," she said warmly. "And I think you're real."

"Recently I haven't even been telling any lies," said Kamil. "Overall I'm becoming better. It's your positive influence. I smile at passers-by instead of kicking their butts. I find women good-looking, men polite, and children well behaved. It's a sign that it's time to be going back."

"Where to?" she asked. "You're the kind of person who has their home everywhere. You don't have to go back anyplace."

"Home," repeated Kamil, and once again felt lonely.

They walked slowly towards the terrace.

Should I tell her, he was thinking, that by her side I'll never be able to weep out those concentration camps and gulags of mine? That that's what it's all about? There aren't any women in the whole world with whom I could weep it all out. Home? What's she talking about? My homes have been burned, my caves closed up, my cabins pulled down.

What is this elegant witch talking about? But let her say what she likes. I thank God she's with me, I can tell her things, I can lie in bed with her, fall asleep by her, just like that. Luckily I'm not one of those guys who talk in their sleep. When I finally fall asleep after the hours of torment, I sleep like a child. Apparently I even look good then. One of them used to tell me that often. One of those who died a long time ago. I don't remember her name. No, I don't think I ever talk in my sleep.

"Do you talk in your sleep?" he asked.

He was standing in the bright light of the lamps in the middle of the terrace. Ruth had disappeared. Gisela had large blue eyes. Right now they were terrified, as if they had seen death. But Gless's eyes did not hold terror. Something had been lit in them that Kamil read as a flicker of reconciliation.

"I think I do sometimes," said Gless.

"I thought so," said Kamil.

"How about you?" asked Gless.

"You should ask a woman about that," said Kamil.

"True," said Gless. "So simple, yet it didn't occur to me."

Kamil felt a rush of liking and regard for this man. Gless was quite tall and had grown somewhat overweight; he had settled on his foundations. Lord Jesus, thought Kamil, he could be my son, and he looks like an old fogey. Who am I? Who actually am I, if in my youth I spawned this nice old man and today almost every night I sleep with his wife? Jesus, of what ore and of what metal did You make me? Out of what terrible lava did You fashion me all those years ago? With what holy water did You fill my veins? And when will I leave at last to find peace in that promised kingdom of Yours?

"What'll you have to drink?" asked Gless.

That happened too, thought Kamil, it all happened once before.

IX

You ask naive questions. What happened when he died? What was supposed to happen, can you tell me that? And what could have happened that day? So my answer is that nothing happened. The day was pretty dull, foggy if I remember right, though I don't think I do remember right as my mind was occupied with something else at the time. For several weeks I'd been in transports of delight over a married woman. That business was even linked to him in a certain way, but at the time I didn't know this. My story doesn't begin till the end of April, a few weeks after the events.

So I think we can safely conclude that on the day he died nothing happened. That, by the way, is typical of your views, Ruth. I'm coming more and more to the conviction that you people here take an amazingly turgid, theatrical approach to the past. When something happened that many years later turned out to have been important, you think that at the moment that event took place there must have been an eclipse of the sun or whatever. But it's never like that. I feel in my bones that I've always learned about the significance of an event the next day or the following week, or a few years later. At the moment that will later be considered critical, nothing happens. People are at a turning point in history, but they don't know it, they go on eating their soup and it doesn't even spill over the side of the bowl.

He died. He was old, so there came a day when he died. Of course, at that time there were people who associated it with the end of the world or something. I wasn't one of them. I adored my married woman, I hurried to her every morning when her husband left for work. I hadn't the faintest idea who her husband was, and some time later that was my downfall. They had a nice *Sezession* apartment, tall decorative stoves, rugs, there was even a cabinet containing priceless porcelain. That husband of hers had no place among the kinds of people who collect porcelain or old silver—he was a primitive boor and a villain; so all the things in the apartment had probably been stolen. A few years before he'd simply gone round to various people, all those frightened doctors, lawyers, and businessmen from before the war, and had asked them politely, with a smile, or even without a smile, to share with him their silver, porcelain, stamp collections, rugs, because he'd like to have nice things too, but he didn't have any nice things like that, yet there's a revolution going on, during revolutions things happen, good things and bad things, so think it over, pal, and in this way he came by the fine objects that I would later see in his home.

These observations should have made me think at the time, but I was still very young and green, and I paid no attention to trifles. It's only years afterwards that a person realizes it's the small details that are crucial.

Over the desk, in a room full of beautiful objects, on the wall hung a photograph of Stalin. That should have made me think too, but it didn't.

It was in that very room that Stalin watched all the fun and games that the lady of the house and I got up to on the small sofa. She was a nice person, not too good-looking, not too bright, but she had two strange traits that were strongly connected in her character: She was an extremely religious woman and at the same time she was extremely excitable sexually.

I'm not just talking about her moralizing remarks, which she uttered almost daily as I stood on the doorstep. She would greet me all in tears, her hair disheveled, her eyes full of metaphysical fervor. She would say feverishly that her sins were terrible ones. This had unpredictable consequences, for at the least appropriate moments she would utter religious exclamations, or for example she would pray tearfully, asking heaven for forgiveness for the licentious acts she was in the very process of committing, something that by the way it was hard to argue with, because she was indeed extraordinarily refined, inventive, creative, passionate, and even filled with a kind of pride that she would be for me a sexual Michurin, an Einstein of the bed or the couch, that she would think up something that the world had never seen. The world might have seen it in fact, but that Stalin on the wall certainly hadn't, because, as you probably know, he was a brutal, obtuse Georgian, he must have been a real barbarian in bed, he probably beat his women or raped them for a while then had them sent off to the camps, far beyond the Arctic Circle.

So she sometimes used to go through these metaphysical transports. Actually, at times she was quite unbearable, for instance when she would yield to the pangs of conscience that gnawed at her and try to drag me into her disputes with God, as if I didn't have my own disputes with Him that were in all probability more fundamental.

Her dress was usually partly unfastened, which made her even more alluring, for she had full breasts, and her arms were shapely if a little on the plump side. She would stand tearfully at the door and cry out in despair that I was dragging her down into hell, because of me she had committed terrible crimes, her sinful body was not equal to the lofty challenges issued by her soul; she would utter these weird half-prayers of hers even when she was already panting with passion, and if I'd taken her seriously and said that she ought not to cheat on her lawful wedded husband I'd probably have got a smack in the mouth, she was in such a frenzy on that sofa. Then, in moments of sweet fatigue, she would try to convert me. She would say I was too young to yield to the influence of such a corrupt, damned woman, that my soul was pure and worthy of creatures better than her. She was probably right, but during those weeks she was the one I liked, maybe because of that pious hysteria, when it came down to it God never left us for a minute, on that sofa I always had the feeling that there were angels with us in the room, though later it turned out that if there'd been anyone there it had probably only been that goddam Stalin. I'll come back to that in a moment, because it's worth remembering; but there's one more thing I want to emphasize: She was a typical example of the kind of women who experience in love moral anxiety. This happens quite often, perhaps without the hysteria, but it does. . . . There is a foolishness in a woman that is not present in a man, even though to tell the truth I value a woman's mind more highly, I have too great a sense of disgust with my own gender.

Tell me, Ruth, do you, in this Calvinist world of yours, which seems rather stifling to me, lacking any prospect of joy, of happiness, the kind of crazy, hazardous, and yet magnificent ascension into heaven that everyone dreams of, to spend a little time in heaven, come what may afterwards, and it's not only here that that's possible, within four walls, a hotel, a shack, a drawing room, no restrictions, anywhere a person can find the one door that leads to heaven, so tell me, Ruth, does that moral imperative to combine love and principles dwell within you also?

If I'm happier with you now than ever before, I guess it's just because for the first time in years I've met a woman who sleeps with me without pangs of conscience, without that pedagogical perversity that drives a woman to moan at the wrongs that are being committed against a deceived wife or her own deceived husband, or the deceived fatherland, something I've also run across in my time.

But there are also women who believe that there are things that are allowed and things that are not allowed; this always seemed to me to be the most disgusting hypocrisy. That pious lioness of mine under the picture of Stalin was like that for the first fifteen minutes. I could kiss her mouth and her breasts, but I wasn't permitted to kiss her thighs. And not just her thighs. Her feet were also shameful, sinful, forbidden things. Ruth, you're not just beautiful, you're also wise, sensitive, and good. Could you explain to me why it is with certain women, where it comes from, that they put their mouths, as it were, at the disposition of a man, their hands can be kissed too, but their stomach is out of the question, or their breasts, or their back. With such fancies anything is possible, a world of perpetual surprises and uncertainty, this is allowed, this isn't, as if somewhere there existed the boundary of sin and impropriety, as if something were wrong with the human body, which has regions that are consecrated and others that are cursed; I'm not saying this for no reason, it concerns you too, my fair one, for I'm permitted to kiss your mouth but not your knees, and I'd like to ask humbly, I'm entitled to put such questions, what sins can your knees have committed that you exclude them from participation in our love?

Let me come back to my lady with the photograph.

In a word, I was foolish, empty-headed, and reckless. One day I stood as usual on the doorstep, I rang the bell, it was a spring morning, the sun was splendid, the sky blue, the birds were chirping, but the door was opened by the lout about whom I knew too little. He dragged me into the apartment.

My dear, there wouldn't be anything special in this; after all, all over the world a jealous husband is entitled to have a word with his wife's fancy man, even to beat the crap out of him. But in the apartment there were three other men waiting for me, with the mournful faces of veterans, in dark suits, tall, broad-shouldered, silent, three officers of the secret service; for the husband of the lady of my heart turned out to be a major in the famous secret police, if that name still means anything to you. Spring 1953, Stalin's still growing cold in the mausoleum, world imperialism threatening the peaceful construction that was thriving from the Elbe to the Pacific, we were building a better future for humanity, and here all of a sudden I'd attempted a kind of coup d'état, I had betrayed the national interest, Poland would never forgive me for it, a young newcomer of doubtful social provenance was corrupting a woman of the new ruling class, and so in the room with the sofa and the photograph of the Generalissimo there rang out the indignant roar of the working class and the peasantry, the three mournful gentlemen set to work, the husband remained in the dignified role of observer of events, a quarter of an hour later I was taken on a stretcher to the holding cells; the next day I would have to sign a statement saying that I had resisted arrest by the authorities of the people's republic, and that I had tried to escape the punishing arm of socialist justice, which when all was said and done was historical justice.

I'll cut the story short, Ruth.

That woman, my sexual Michurin, turned out to be a decent person. If it weren't for her they'd have broken every bone in my body and I wouldn't have gotten out of prison for two or three years. She knew how to influence her husband, because a few weeks later I was a free man; after that I spent some time in the hospital in the provinces recovering. I never saw the woman or her husband again, nor that lousy city. And on top of it all I profited morally from the experience. I could pass as a political prisoner of those times, something from which various people later benefited considerably. However, I remained an old idiot, and I always told the truth, that I'd been a victim of passion.

But in the end, if there was anything human in that husband of hers, that was it. For a number of weeks I'd stolen his wife away from him; did I have the right later to deprive him of that little bit of Shakespeare with which God had endowed him?

X

"Once, a long time ago, I can't say exactly when, but when I was young, and it's very important that this story took place when I was very young, you should make a note of that . . ."

"I don't need to make a note of it," said Ruth in response. "I'm recording it."

"True. But I'm talking about, referring to, my very distant youth. It may even have been my childhood. I want to emphasize that firmly."

"You said that once already."

"Because I want to emphasize it. That's why. And if you're going to ignore my remarks, certain, you might say, fundamental pointers, then I'd be in favor of calling the whole thing off after all."

"I'm treating this seriously . . ."

"It's not a question of being serious, Ruth. I don't demand seriousness of you, your being serious is worth nothing; what I ask for is proof of loyalty. Am I not entitled to that modicum of loyalty that one person deserves from another? After all, it's about my life and I only had the one, goddammit, so I don't want to lay down unreasonable demands, I just mean that little bit of human solidarity, to be treated like a human being, I mean we're not talking about cats and dogs here, not even about hippopotamuses, but about a particular individual who woman once bore, who suffered once, and I want to know now if I'm expressing myself clearly enough for your intellectual capacities, or whether I should destroy this tape recorder, which, generally speaking, you're more concerned about than about the guy who for some unknown reason you've been talking to for the last few days in this air-conditioned hotel room where even the mice and the roaches drop dead from this Genevan elegance of yours."

"I'm sorry," said Ruth Gless. "I know it's hard, and I do everything I can to make it easier for you. If you like, we could take a break today. It's such a nice sunny day, we could take a trip to Megeve or Sallanche, then we'll get back to work this evening."

"No," said Kamil. "I don't want to run away. There's only one thing I want. It must be noted that this took place in my early youth. It was during the war. Otherwise everything will turn out to be meaningless."

"Okay," said Ruth. "I'm recording now. This takes place in wartime. Right?"

"Yes," said Kamil. "But I don't remember when it was. I was a boy. I was eligible for forced labor. Do you know what forced labor is?"

"There is research on that subject," said Ruth. "I'm writing it down. Forced labor."

"Right. Actually, it's fairly simple. Hitler said *Arbeit*

macht frei. Work makes you free. While Stalin said, He who doesn't work doesn't eat. So here you have two versions. The romantic and the pragmatic. Do you understand, Ruth?"

"I understand the words. I understand the words, but I know that's not enough."

"That's a lot," interrupted Kamil. "I know people who don't even understand the words. And they try to convince others that they have the patent on being right from the Lord God Himself."

"What about the idea of Megeve? You've never seen Mont Blanc. It's only one afternoon."

"I've never seen angels either, but I believe they exist. Mont Blanc can stay where it is. We'll meet each other in good time. It's good that you understand the words. I love you, Ruth, for that modesty of yours. That's the best thing you could give me. And that's what you do give me. I'm going to smoke my pipe now. But let's not stop the recording.

"So it's wartime. A woman in wartime. Not a mother, not a lover, not a sister, not a Polish woman, not a Jewish woman in wartime. And yet a woman of those times. A German woman in wartime. That's important, Ruth. A German woman who was my first experience in wartime. I was a boy then. I had to work real hard. One day a German woman, tall, big, with blond hair and horsey teeth, when she smiled she exposed her pink gums and looked particularly hideous; this woman, then, the wife of the local policeman, who was known for his brutality, called me to her house and ordered me to take a big, heavy wardrobe up to the third floor. She called a boy, I was a boy then, I was twelve or thirteen, just a child, and she ordered me to haul that wardrobe up the stairs; and I carried it upstairs. It took me almost half the day. I went up those stairs step by step, step by step, step by step, for hours, for hours I dragged that fearful wardrobe behind me, it was the biggest wardrobe in the entire world, I tell you, half of Europe could have fitted into that wardrobe, and I dragged it up to the third floor, one step at a time, one inch at a time, blinded by sweat, I couldn't breathe, I was blind, deaf, and dumb, I was a fish on the sand, I was a sparrow at the bottom of the sea. Just think, Ruth, I was twelve, a little boy, thin arms, frail legs, weak hands, a little boy, little more than a child, and that wardrobe the size of the Third Reich, or perhaps even bigger, a warm day, maybe sunny even, the stairs of an apartment building, me on those stairs, a boy with a wardrobe, and in the meantime the world continued to exist, life went on happening, someone died, someone else was just being born, maybe right then Hitler was having a migraine, maybe Stalin was having an asthma attack, who would know now, at least you weren't alive at that time, and I thank God that you weren't, nothing special was happening, I mean at that time people were dying like flies, in the east and in the west they were dying like flies, in the hundreds of thousands, and in the middle of Europe me, with that goddam wardrobe, step after step, drop of sweat after drop of sweat, stair after stair, hour after hour, dragging my lousy fate.

"But it wasn't that that I wanted to tell you about. Because in the end, just quite how I don't know myself, I dragged that wardrobe to the top, and the German woman said that it was in the right place, that it was where it was supposed to be. Then she took me by the hand like a good mother and led me downstairs, and then along a long dark corridor to the garden. It was an orchard, Ruth. There were apple trees, pear trees, plum trees, there might even have been cherry trees; all the little trees had white trunks, and their tops were covered in blossoms. It was a warm summer's afternoon. And then the German woman said some words to me that I didn't understand, yet I did. She said I should have a rest because I was tired. And she told me to lie down on the grass under the fruit trees. And I lay down, and I stayed there till dusk. And I felt the earth, the air, the world, and I felt life. As never before and never after I felt my body, there wasn't as much of it as a growing lad might have, how much of his own body might he have? I tell you, Ruth. I had then more body than today, than both of us today, than everyone in the whole world. Have you ever felt your body to such an extent that you know simultaneously that you have arms, legs, shoulders, a head, feet, buttocks, that you have lungs, a heart, a liver, that all of that is a person, that that is the whole person, made up of such wonderful different parts, and that each part is together and is separate, and all this is a gift from the Lord God, who is looking down at you, smiling and telling you to lie a while longer, you have time till sundown, that German woman will bring you a slice of bread and a cup of cold milk, wait a while longer, she's bound to bring it to you, it is I who am telling you, boy, your Lord God, who delivered you from slavery in the land of Egypt. And she did indeed

bring bread and jam, milk, cheese, and also an R-6 cigarette, and finally she said that I'd done a good job of setting
up the wardrobe.

"And now, Ruth, my love, tell me, do there still exist
such huge wardrobes, such grass, trees, and clouds like the
ones that were passing over me then, when I opened my
eyes like a dead man suddenly and unexpectedly brought
back to life?

"And I'll tell you one more thing, Ruth, and then we
can even go to Megeve if you fancy. Let me tell you that I
remember that wardrobe with love. Thanks to it I learned
what a person's body is. Maybe that's why I don't feel like
going to Megeve now. Maybe that's why I'd like to fall
asleep by you, Ruth, in your good arms, and you will watch
over me.

"And if I die, it will be peacefully, for there'll be someone with me who will wash my limbs and then lay them in
my casket."

XI

If the subject of the Jews is indispensable in my recordings, that won't be a problem. After all, I come from the homeland of all the Jews on earth, though there are some among them who won't admit it, quite the opposite even, they emphasize ostentatiously that they're from Chile or Zaire, which must be a great source of amusement for any real Jew, for among real Jews it's common knowledge that it is only in the last half century that the state of Israel has introduced disorder into the Jewish genealogical tree, which had been flourishing for centuries. In the history of the Jewish people there are only two chapters: In the first there appear famous names such as Moses, King David, Nebuchadnezzar, the Prophets, and the Judges; while in the second chapter, without any reason or explanation, yet most convincingly, there suddenly appear the cities of Garwolin, Tarnów, Białystok, and a hundred other Polish towns where all the Jews of the world had gathered.

But from the time of Adolf Hitler the Jews no longer lived there, as the great majority of them had been murdered, while those who had managed to make it through the Holocaust alive had barely a quarter of a century of peace ahead of them, because then there appeared General Moczar and his Neanderthal squads.

It's that time that I want to talk about now, because it was then that two pretty women played an important role in my crazy life.

They called her Fedora, heaven knows why; I met her in an upstairs nightclub somewhere in Katowice, crimson-colored stairs, gilt, there was an old gray-haired woman in the cloakroom, herring with sour cream in the buffet, and a bartender in a tuxedo, I remember that, it was the year of the great revenge of the Polish nation upon its Jewish oppressors, General Moczar was organizing camps for academics, writers, and journalists, certain patriots even began riding horses to be different and offer proof of their unquestioned Aryan identity, for when all's said and done what Jew could ever stay up on a horse, goddammit, so it was that memorable year, students to their studies, writers to their pens, and Zionists to Siam, that was when I met Fedora, I remember now, that was her stage name, a guy used to come out on the little stage and say, And now, ladies and gentlemen, may I present our magnificent Fedora, and she would appear, all in tulle, as great and thrilling as the Brothers Karamazov, she would dance and sing, maybe something in French since Piaf was in vogue then, so Fedora was Piaf too, basically a good-looking woman, somehow honest and fresh despite the dust and filth of the clubs where she'd been singing for years, by then she was already really afraid, it may well have been partly out of fear that she went with me, maybe she was frightened of me, after all I was a stranger from Warsaw, the memorable year of the great settling of accounts, and she was no longer a child, quite the opposite, she had half a century under her belt, she knew which side her bread was buttered on, she'd spent the war in Kraków as a cook for some German business-man, he probably used to rape her twice a week, in that memorable year of reckonings once more, after a long break, she became Jewish again, for there is a time when each person returns to that which was preordained for them, whether they want to or not, so she wasn't as attrac-tive as once before, but legends were recounted about her thighs, that was what tempted me then, it really was worthy of an epic poem, to the extent that when a little while later Fedora came to Warsaw to leave forever the homeland of her non-Aryan ancestors and travel to the Promised Land, or maybe just to Düsseldorf, at the risk of being called a shabbes goy, which I have essentially been all my life, I saw my Fedora off at the Gdańsk Station, and as she was pulling out, leaning out of the window with tears streaming down her face, I shouted to her in rage, powerlessness, and humil-iation, Take care, Fedora, with thighs like those you don't need to worry about any partisans . . .

In those days, I spent a fair amount of time generally at vari-ous train stations and also at Warsaw airport. I used to have many Jewish friends and acquaintances; at that time they were leaving Poland, traveling somewhere else, traveling, traveling, as far as possible from Poland. Various things happened at those partings; there was often a lot of crying, for Jews and Poles are awfully sentimental people.

It was October, early in the afternoon, the sky was glassy, bright, cloudless, like the dome of some temple, the platforms were deserted, just a few Jewish families, masses of luggage, on that last journey they were taking all their life's possessions, at this time certain Poles recalled the days of war, here and there they ripped off those poor Jews, the customs officials and the security service gorillas, though ready neighbors were also to be found, generally speaking the city looked strange then, troglodytes out on the streets, I don't think decent people went out of their homes at all, or perhaps it was the case that my nation simply showed its true face at that time.

So that October I had come to the platform to say goodbye to the Zylbersztajns.

I'll tell you who Zylbersztajn was. He was a Warsaw Jew who had miraculously survived the war behind a wardrobe in a town outside the city, where he was hidden by the clerks from the store he had owned before the war. After the war he worked as the chief accountant in a state foot-wear factory. And as the chief accountant he suddenly turned out to be the right hand of Dayan and Golda Meir. When I arrived on the platform, Dayan's right-hand man was sitting on three battered suitcases reading a newspaper in which it was written that he was Dayan's right-hand man.

Next to Zylbersztajn and his three battered suitcases stood Mrs. Zylbersztajn, and it was she who was my main problem in those historic times.

On that platform there came to a momentous end something that had begun in banal fashion a few years before in a Warsaw nightclub.

I'll tell you the story, including certain details, for never in my life have such apparently tiny details played such a major role.

So I was sitting at the bar, because I like sitting at bars, over the bar there's usually a mirror in which you can see what's going on behind you, no surprises, nothing unexpected, so I'm sitting at the bar and all of a sudden in the mirror I see an incredibly beautiful woman. A dusky brunette, her hair brushed smooth and parted in the middle, eyes as black as in Russian romances, a profile from a cameo, a woman built magnificently, what you might call the Lord God's most impressive architecture.

She was dancing with a little dark guy, but in fact she was dancing on her own, in marvelous concentration, engrossed in the music and in her own internal rhythm, her eyes were half-closed, her lips slightly parted, the eyes of every man in the club were glued on her, she danced very lightly, effortlessly, I stared at her legs, they were like space, they went on infinitely, superbly slender, small feet in stiletto heels, the shoes were silver, her dress was turquoise, generally speaking she dressed somewhat extravagantly, she often used to wear huge clip-on earrings, lots of jewelry, there was something about her of the high-class hooker, something provocative, nonchalant, erotic, she was always encased in a neurotic aura, that's important in my story.

But let me return to that first night; naturally I couldn't pass up such an opportunity, an hour later I was already dancing with her and I already knew that she wanted the same thing, in such situations no words are needed, a breath is sufficient, a touch, a look, and that was exactly how it began then, the next day I was at her place, and while chief accountant Zylbersztajn was swindling the Polish state on behalf of the footwear factory, Mrs. Zylbersztajn was making love with me in indescribable ways.

Incidentally, that doesn't often happen, because very beautiful women rarely belong to the most erotic class, I think some imperfection is needed, something lacking to make a woman seek compensation and find it in love, but Zylbersztajn's wife was the exception, and for that reason I won't go on about this, I'll just say briefly that I lost my head over her, she enthralled me, and that's all there is to it. A few months later, the beginning of winter, the first frosts, nice December days, snow creaking underfoot, a kind of purity in the air, a kind of peace in my heart, I was replete, I was proud, I might even have been happy, for the first time in years, just then, one day the telephone rings, and when I pick up the receiver it's Zylbersztajn, whom I don't actually know at all, about whom I know only that he exists, that he's a chief accountant, and that his wife cheats on him with me almost daily, so Zylbersztajn is calling me, and in an exceedingly polite voice he asks to meet with me. I'm flattered, Mr. Zylbersztajn, I reply, but do we in fact know each other? No, we don't, he says, but we could get to know each other, it won't take long, I'd just like to have a few words with you, at five o'clock this afternoon I'll be waiting at the Melpomena café, the table to the left by the door, I'm quite short, I'm wearing a gray suit, just in case I'll be carrying a copy of Hemingway's *For Whom the Bell Tolls*, because I really love that book, and besides, I think the bell may be tolling for me right now. With that he ended the conversation.

That afternoon at five I walk into the Melpomena café, at the table on the left is sitting a thin little Jew, before him lies the Hemingway, I sit right next to Zylbersztajn on an uncomfortable chair, we order coffee, I fill my pipe and light it carefully, then Zylbersztajn speaks in a very quiet, calm yet perhaps ever so slightly perturbed voice, that he loves his wife very much, she means the world to him, do I understand that, do I realize that a woman is the whole world for a man, but what Zylbersztajn is saying puts me in a rather difficult position, because then, in the Melpomena café, I have no notion of that, I had never met a woman like that, since even Mrs. Zylbersztajn was not the whole world for me, maybe an important little part of it, maybe an adornment of it, maybe its point, but when it came down to it apart from her there existed other matters, at that time I couldn't foresee my future, I couldn't meet my own destiny

ahead of time and tell Zylbersztajn that yes indeed, I know
that feeling, when a man has a woman and expects nothing
more of God, because he has everything, all the trees and all
the clouds, damnation and redemption at the same time, at
that time I was ignorant of all that, and so I treated Zylbersztajn's outpourings with a certain skepticism, that of course
I understand everything, Mr. Zylbersztajn, I've heard it ru-
mored that your wife is a beautiful woman, and then he
said that I shouldn't make jokes at his expense, he's an old
man, he's been through a great deal in his life, he knows all
about me, he hesitated for a long time whether to ask me
for this talk, in the end he made his mind up, because in
this he sees his last chance, he had a choice between this
talk and death in pain and despair, that's exactly how he
put it, he repeated it twice, stirring his coffee with a spoon,
My good sir, I had a choice between this talk and death in
pain and despair. And I think it was then, when he uttered
those astonishing words for the second time, that something finally got through to me, like a ray of light, something that paralyzed me, like what a person experiences
when they're woken in the middle of the night by the powerful beam of an electric flashlight, though I now know it
was a light from my future, a second of self-knowledge, a
ray of my own despair and my own pain, sent from those
years that had not yet come to pass, that were still ahead,
and then I told Zylbersztajn not to say any more, It's true, I
said, your wife and I are close, but now I feel very bad,
please hear me out, Mr. Zylbersztajn, I'm terribly sorry
about this, but since we're already talking so openly, with
some pain, with some despair, then you should know that

she is very dear to me, she is loved by me, Mr. Zylbersztajn, at this he gave a smile, a soft, gentle, melancholy smile such as only old Jews can smile, and he said that that was understandable, who wouldn't love Mrs. Zylbersztajn, once he gets to know her well, but he wanted to stress as strongly as he could that no one loved her like he, Zylbersztajn, did, and for that reason he entreated me not to have anything more to do with this woman, you're much younger than me, he said, there are so many women in the world who will bring you happiness, contentment, maybe even good fortune, but I'm a tired old Jew, once I had a family, I had a good, pretty wife, I had children too, a son and a daughter, I was a man who didn't complain, of course life had buffeted me, in Poland could it have been otherwise, but everything seemed to pan out more or less, I had a small business, a stationery shop, I liked those goods, they were clean, nice, decent goods, a little bit of culture in those dark times, pencils to write with, crayons for children to draw trees, houses, and sky, exercise books, pencil cases, but, well, you know what happened, the Germans murdered my whole family, I managed to survive thanks to some good people, then came this new Poland, I was getting by somehow, suffering somehow, and in the end I met this woman, so beautiful, so kind, so good, she strokes my brow at night when I cry out in my sleep, she didn't live through as much, so she is forbearing with me, it's very nice to hear that you love her, but I love her more and I need her more than you do, so I'm asking you, I'm appealing to your integrity, to your honor, you're a Pole, for you honor still means something, end this friendship, my wife will get over it somehow, it will hurt her but life always hurts a little, so it will pass, please tell me now that you won't see her any more.

I promised Zylbersztajn everything he wanted, I stood and left the Melpomena, and he stayed behind and went on listening to the bell tolling for him.

I remember I went straight to the train station, bought a ticket to Gdańsk, got in the train, and traveled for several hours in an empty, poorly lit compartment, with my head wrapped in my overcoat, and I wept from sorrow at the loss of Mrs. Zylbersztajn. At the station in Gdańsk I had a few beers, ate something hot, and then got back on the train to return to Warsaw through the dark, frosty night. On the way back I stopped crying and thought over what I'd talked about with Zylbersztajn. I was becoming more and more convinced that I'd been deceived by a sly old Jew who had trapped me with the bait of sympathy.

Who said he loved more than I did? And why was I supposed to sacrifice my intense feelings for Mrs. Zylbersztajn, especially considering the fact that she didn't love her husband at all, quite the opposite, she often used to tell me that she'd had it up to here with that old Jew, whereas to me she gave continual displays of very passionate love.

When I reached Warsaw and got off the train it was three in the morning, the frost nipped at my face, the streets were almost completely deserted, I walked briskly home, and the next day I already knew that I would call beautiful Mrs. Zylbersztajn.

I thought with a certain satisfaction, even with a sense of sweet revenge, that only a stupid Jew could imagine it was a matter of honor. In this world there aren't any matters of honor between a man and a woman, and this was a matter between me and Mrs. Zylbersztajn, not her husband.

And of course it went on. I thought that Zylbersztajn no longer knew what was going on, even more, for after some time he called me and invited me to have dinner at his home. I expressed considerable surprise, I even tried to get out of it, but he insisted rather firmly, he said that everything was okay, the problems were over, why not give oneself a treat, his wife mentioned me from time to time, warmly and fondly, while he trusted me like he trusted himself, after all dinner is only dinner, you must come, don't disappoint us. I went, feeling lousy, the small apartment, I sat at the table, ate roast, and through the open door I could see in the next room the sofa on which the day before the lady of the house and I had been making love till we were breathless, for she was very boisterous in love.

Later on Zylbersztajn repeated his invitation, it was disagreeable and onerous for me, but whenever I tried to refuse he would make strange comments, Are you afraid of my wife, he would ask with a touch of derision, What are you apprehensive about, it's a closed matter, it's in the past, so please don't refuse, besides, I feel more at ease when I have my eye on you, that was what he would say to me, so I would yield to his requests, or rather his pressure, I virtually became a member of the household, in the morning I would drop in for some moments of erotic transport,

in the evening for a chat with Zylbersztajn, it was all rather
disgusting, the woman amazed me, she gave the impression
that she was terribly pleased, at times she would behave in a
most provocative way, once she started to kiss me next to
an open door beyond which sat Zylbersztajn, I heard his
cough, I could almost feel his breath on my shoulder, What
are you doing, Tamara, I whispered, but what could I say,
she always had that effect on me, so I kissed her in that
room, by the half-open door, virtually in his presence.

There came a day when Nasser made up his mind to kill off
all the Jews, but the Jews kicked the Egyptians' butts, and in
Warsaw General Moczar decided that his hour had come.
The communists in Poland took it upon themselves to
avenge the honor of the pharaohs, General Moczar may
even have said to his minions that forty centuries were
looking down upon them.

In any case the Jews began to leave, because Poland had
become unbearable for them. For many Poles it had also
become unbearable, but unfortunately the Poles couldn't
leave, they had to stay and go on loving their homeland.

In this way Zylbersztajn found himself on the platform with
his wife and three suitcases. By this stage we'd long been on
first-name terms, we often used to play chess in the evening, while Tamara served us tea and jam, like in the good
old days, in the nineteenth century.

The train arrived on time and the moment of parting came.
I kissed Tamara on the hand and on both cheeks, I had

tears in my eyes, this time it really was the end, they would never again return to this city, to this country where they were born, where they lived all the years of their lives, and now they had suddenly become exiles, terrible moments that other people in the world are incapable of imagining, and then Zylbersztajn told me in a very quiet, very grave tone to take Tamara in my arms, to kiss her the way a loving man kisses a beloved woman, it was important for the three of us, he said, I'm no stupid Jew, you were the stupid one, Kamil, do you think I haven't known about you for ages, do you think that through all those years I was deaf and blind, I was not deaf or blind in the slightest but I was far-sighted and provident, she's not a woman for whom my love could be enough, she deserved more, a better fate than merely Jewish wrongs, Jewish phantoms, a Jewish accountant, she was entitled to more, such a beautiful woman, so full of delicacy and yearnings, if you hadn't been by her side there would have been another, another one, a second, maybe a third, so any sensible man in my place would have acted likewise, don't look at me like that, Kamil, it's true that at the moment I feel a touch of satisfaction, I really wasn't any more foolish than the two of you, but let's forgive each other everything, this really is the end between us, take her in your arms now, kiss her passionately, with the greatest love you can muster, let her take that Polish kiss of yours with her into her future life, she won't have any Polish kisses any more, something is coming to an end, never to return, this stupid Poland did after all give her a little love, a little joy, with you, so stop pretending, everything's behind us now, that was what Zylbersztajn said then, and I did what he asked, I took Tamara in my arms, I kissed her passionately, and he sat calmly on the suitcases and watched, Tamara was crying loudly, I could taste her tears on my lips, those were our dead kisses, the fearful ashes of love, the empty platform, around us an evil, hostile, villainous city, an old Jew on suitcases, a woman in my arms, and me, indescribably alone, cruelly cheated, then they both got on the train, I helped them stow their suitcases in the compartment, Tamara stood by the window, her face bathed in tears, and next to her stood Zylbersztajn, somehow dignified, noble, strong, suddenly he seemed tall, almost as tall as his wife, he put his arm around her as a sign that he was now taking possession of her for good, now he would be her guardian, husband, lover, her shield and support, the train moved off, I stood on the empty platform, thinking, thinking, thinking in despair that from now on that goddam bell would be tolling only for me.

XII

"I don't mean to cause trouble," said Gauting. "And I'm not trying to be rude; it's just that the matter has got a little complicated, which is why I'm here."

Gauting was wearing a very stylish cherry-red blazer bearing the crest of a nonexistent club, gabardine trousers, cherry-red golfing shoes, and a Versace necktie; he smelt of Eau Sauvage and had blond hair that was turning a little gray. His eyes gazed watchfully from behind not especially thick glasses in frames the color of dark honey. Gauting was tall and slim; he held himself straight, he had bony hands on which grew small tufts of dark hair, generally speaking he was pretty macho, he had thick stubble, his chest was full, his hips were narrow for his age, and his shoulders were broad, he had a strong, fit figure, the eye of a wildcat, with a yellowish gleam, cold for men and glowing for pretty women, in a word a fine individual, a good hundred fifty pounds of gentleman, who would only need one smack in the face to spend the next two weeks whimpering and wagging his tail when he saw you.

"Mr. Gauting is in charge of the whole series," said Ruth. "We've just been reviewing some of your recordings."

"And how do you find them?" asked Kamil politely. "I hope smoking's allowed in here."

"Not really," said Gauting courteously, "but we make an exception for our guests."

"I thought so." Kamil began to fill his pipe.

It was a small, plain, dark room, probably a little-used recording studio, because Kamil could see through a broad window into the technician's control room next door. Inside three guys in jeans and sweaters were tinkering with the equipment.

"I'm all ears," said Kamil.

"I've listened to some of the recordings," said Gauting. "And I don't think this is what we had in mind during our initial talks."

"I don't think so either," said Kamil. "You've summoned a false witness."

"I want to stress that what you have to say is interesting. I really do like it. But as far as our series is concerned, things should go in a different direction. We have nothing against our guests giving various details from their lives, for we're keen to convey the true feel of events, but at bottom, you yourself understand, we're aiming to collect testimonies of the times, testimonies of the changes."

"What is it I understand?" asked Kamil, lighting his pipe carefully.

"It's a question of the kind of accounts that most clearly illuminate the great changes. The world experienced the fall of the communist system, and you participated in it personally, you lived through those radical transformations day by day, so we're interested in a record of your feelings and thoughts at that time, what your reactions were, what you thought would happen, what you expected, what disappointments you encountered, in what ways your life changed, I don't want to resort to cliches . . ."

"Precisely," said Kamil. "Then don't. I've already said you have a false witness here. I'm not the right guy. You mentioned something about communism, if I heard right?"

"I did," acknowledged Gauting.

"Under communism I was younger, Mr. Gauting. The women were younger then too. You were probably younger also, though maybe you didn't realize it. Mrs. Gless and I have talked at some length about these matters."

"Yes," said Ruth in an animated voice, "we've talked exhaustively about that."

"You have quite a sense of humor," put in Gauting tartly.

"Yes, that's right," said Kamil. "And so I want to make a suggestion. Could those lads on the other side of the window record our conversation? For posterity, exactly like you want, Mr. Gauting."

"Of course," agreed Gauting with sudden alacrity.

"Then have them start recording. This time just for the archives."

"This was precisely what I had in mind when I invited you to the studio. To record something in a different style. And I'm delighted."

"Good," said Kamil.

"Are you set, Jean Claude?" Gauting asked after turning on the microphone.

A young guy in a green sweater nodded.

"Then we can begin recording, my good sir," said Gauting cordially.

Ruth shook her head slightly. On her pretty, somewhat weary face there appeared a trace of uneasiness.

"Is there any point in this?" she asked quietly.

"My dear lady," exclaimed Gauting.

A red light went on.

"Do you think we can begin?" asked Kamil.

"Yes," said Gauting. "We most certainly can."

Mr. Gauting, said Kamil into the microphone. It's worth clearing up a few misunderstandings, since there won't be another opportunity. I want to emphasize that I'm an ordinary person, the average man in the street, like the vast majority of people in this best of all possible worlds. What is it that interests a simple person, what do you think, my dear Mr. Gauting? Is a simple person interested in the unification of Europe, or the intimate relations linking Beijing and Moscow, and Moscow and Washington? I assure you that the only intimate relations that excite that gentleman who's working the tape recorder right now are those between himself and his wife or his lover. Furthermore, the same applies to you, Mr. Gauting. It's enough to look closely at your necktie to see that women play a huge role in your godless life. Has this microphone been switched off yet? I confess that I don't count in the slightest on your forbearance. Yet I think I deserve a little courtesy. I won't talk for long, Mr.

Gauting, because whatever happens I don't think we'd ever come to any agreement on this issue. I just want to draw your attention to a number of seemingly trivial matters. It seems to me that you're suffering from a typical western complex of spiritual poverty. You share the view, universal here, that people such as me, who have been ground in the merciless mills of totalitarian regimes, have through that torment come to enjoy some kind of extraordinary wealth in their inner lives. You've been deluded into thinking that suffering counts as spiritual experience, and that the evil a person encounters makes them more complete inside.

It's my belief that you're mistaken. In my country you can also find people who think like you. They believe that life in such a stable world, for example here in Geneva, is unbearable, because here everything can be foreseen, here there are no surprises, mysteries, disappointments, and thus there are also no dramas, as if to have drama you had to have surprises or the idiocies and crimes of communist tyranny.

There is in you, Mr. Gauting, a desire that has never been properly expressed, never been given its proper name, a desire to try your strength against the suffering you were spared, because it's a tempting and unknown suffering, something exciting, that was probably how the travelers of old felt as they set off on stormy oceans, where there awaited them things that were terrible because they were unknown, cruel because they were foreign, devilish because they were distant.

You know your angels, Mr. Gauting, you've counted the feathers on each of their wings a hundred times, but never, this is how you think, never in your path have you encountered a real devil. I wouldn't be so certain of that, my dear Mr. Gauting, but if you've never met a devil, then you should please thank God and not undertake any dangerous endeavors. Survive, Mr. Gauting, survive and thank God. And give up these longings, listen to what I truly have to say to you, your children, and your children's children.

You drew a better straw, and I drew a worse one. Please, finally respect that, and finally acknowledge it. That's the only thing I can ask of you, the only favor that people like you can do for those like me: to finally stop talking about our experiences.

I'm speaking of a little bit of respect and trust. If I repeat that the sufferings brought about by totalitarian regimes of various hues do not constitute any form of spiritual wealth, please believe me, for I know what I'm talking about.

And if I tell you that only love is worth anything in a person's life, then don't expect from me any outpourings about communism or Nazi concentration camps, because I want to talk about the real person, who has legs, arms, shoulders, fingers, nose, eyes, hair, feet, tongue, who thinks and feels, I want to speak of the person between light and shadow, sound and silence, cold and heat, in a word about someone who is quite simply alive, and you're trying to foist off on me my mutilated body, severed limbs and bloody stumps, so that from it I might extract for you the riches of the human soul. But here there are no riches, believe me.

And if someone comes to you from those parts, from that accursed land of mine, if someone comes and says that he bears riches, just throw him down the stairs, my dear Mr. Gauting, for he will be a cheat and a dissembler.

Now I'll tell you something that seems to me to be of particular importance. I wish you all well and I want to disabuse you of an error that for decades has been lingering in your honest souls. Listen, Mr. Gauting. In Geneva you may have a gulag such as was never dreamed of even in Vorkuta. Have you ever stood at dusk on a poorly lit street and stared at the one and only window in the entire world, in which the light has just been turned off? And you know why the light went out and you know what the darkness is for, Mr. Gauting. If you have had a similar experience, then you've done five years in Kolyma, or five years in Buchenwald. And if you've lived through a night of fearful dread such as God can bring down upon a person, a night of waiting for your beloved woman, who has humiliated you or abandoned you or made a laughingstock of you, or stopped loving you, then you've already been on the scaffold where Robespierre gave his head, and you've been where those from the resistance died, and finally you've been where innocent passers-by perished on a Warsaw street.

Though it may sound like heresy, I'll say what I think. I think that in any cosy little house where two people live, it's possible at a given time to cross the threshold to the gas chamber. Mr. Gauting, if you wish to save yourself, don't ask God for democracy, a free market economy, interest rates, and prosperity in Zaire; ask that God spare you unhappy love.

You keep asking me about totalitarianism. About those experiences. I'll say only that there's nothing I managed to salvage. There's nothing I was able to carry to the other side. And there's nothing that is worth regretting. And there's nothing that should be missed.

Everything that has any value I carry within myself, Mr. Gauting, and that is nothing but the memory of a man's love for a woman, requited or unrequited, betrayed or spurned, trampled upon or given wings. To finish, I'll tell you something sad, though it may give you strength. When Jesus hung on the cross and had stopped breathing, when He had already passed away, His thirst quenched with vinegar, pierced with a spear, when the sun went down and that terrible night fell, and neither moon nor any stars appeared in the sky, for God in His heaven was suffering in sorrow and pain, weeping bitterly at the death of His only son, and He could not move arm or leg, so empty was He and so burned up by despair, what was left then beneath that cross, Mr. Gauting? What was left beneath the cross, aside from love?

XIII

This is a very sad story, but I think Mr. Gauting would be pleased. It's a pity, then, he had to leave us so suddenly to travel overseas. In general I get the impression that you're not exactly home-lovers here. Appearances to the contrary. Because where I come from there are various funny stories about you, probably from the eighteenth century, when you really did live in a closed, inaccessible country, protected by the mountains and by the manly breasts of your soldiers, who were prepared to die in defense of the Confederation. But today, I guess, you've already joined that great nation of nomads driven by something or other, anywhere so long as it's away from your own four walls, away from your home town.

That is an admirable trait in people today; I can see clear as day that determined effort to escape from the fate that is constantly at your heels, catching up with you at the least expected moment, for instance in the Antipodes, or in

Veracruz, where our good Mr. Gauting is currently gathering material for an edifying little piece about the tribula-
tions of Mexico.

I'm not being sarcastic, my dear Jean Claude, don't smile so
knowingly, I'm made of the same clay, I'd also really like to
bend sympathetically over someone else's misfortune.
How much joy and satisfaction it brings, how it strengthens
one's fragile belief in the rationality of the way things are.
For if Gauting is deeply touched as he passes through the
narrow, squalid alleyways of Latin America, he'll also be
accompanied by a slightly embarrassing yet sweet conviction that here in Geneva, for decades people have worked
better, more dependably, more honestly, and that we have
the results to show for it. Because once the Lord God
comes up with something and sets His mind on it, it will
always be done wisely.

I think that's what Gauting believes, and you too, my dear
Jean Claude, and if you, beautiful Mrs. Gless, are prey to
similar delusions, that means I've not yet managed to corrupt you sufficiently, but I most definitely will, just don't
begrudge me the time.

I have my reasons for talking about all this, because I remember today's sad story precisely as an example of the
wise designs of the Lord God, which in practice turned out
after all to be a totally botched job. To tell the truth, I like
experiences such as this, because they permit me to cherish
the hope that the Lord God is also a Pole, that He thinks

wisely but acts unwisely, that His intentions are often of the best, but whatever He turns His hand to falls apart, frequently with lamentable consequences.

Are you recording already, Jean Claude? Excellent; Mrs. Gless, why don't you move your seat a little, I'd like to be able to see you in the control room, I've become accustomed to your being close during our recordings, shifting them to the studio really isn't such a good idea, so I'm hoping that we'll go back to our tête-à-têtes, where I can draw strength from your gentle looks, please take that confession at face value, and you, dear Jean Claude, understand what I mean, Mrs. Gless has a soothing effect on me, for when you talk of bad things, you feel the need to have good people close to you, don't you agree, Jean Claude. There you are, it's really very straightforward.

So, my fair lady, thank you for that, and now please sit more to the right, nearer to the console, yes, right there, now I can see you clearly, it's important to me, Mrs. Gless, dear Ruth. And please forgive me, please forgive me. Think of me as if I were a poor, narrow, crowded alleyway in Veracruz. Then the world will right itself.

That evening a severe frost set in. This may seem nothing special, but after several weeks of what appeared to be all the winter we would have, when people had already come to believe that at least nature had given them a reprieve, had gone easy on them, something that they would never have expected from the Polish state in those days, all of a sudden a fearful winter descended upon the city, the like of which hadn't been seen in years. The frost intensified almost from hour to hour, footsteps sounded on the icy sidewalks, the dark streets of Warsaw became even more deserted, everyone took shelter in those absurd, cramped, dirty apartments, where after a few hours people were moving about like Mongolian shepherds in their desert yurts, blankets around their shoulders, caps on their heads, because the socialist state hadn't had the foresight to anticipate the possibility of frost in December, so the radiators were barely working, turned right down, the temperature was plummeting, people were drinking hot tea, going to bed, covering themselves up to the ears, hugging each other, that frost may even have reconciled the occasional couple who had fallen out, in a word God, who had meant well, had wanted to please the children with a little snow before Christmas, to paint a few frost flowers on the window panes to beautify that dark, ugly city, had messed up again and made things easier for the devil.

In fact, the whole thing was going to be the night of the devil, but at eight in the evening, as the harsh frost was setting in, hardly anyone in Warsaw or in Poland knew it.

Those were very sad days for me, because I'd just broken up with a nice, cultured woman who'd had a soothing effect on me, and I was needing more and more to be soothed, I was already fifty, and I'd become ponderous; I had a fondness for comforts, and an aversion to youth, which had been taken away from me while others still possessed it and even boasted about it, a kind of weariness with life, with women, with myself, a weariness that heralded the first serious thoughts about death, and they were no longer the rather melodramatic thoughts of a young man, when you want to die out of spite, or because of some trifle like the absurdity of existence, but mature and bitter thoughts, when you know already that the whole meaning lies in coping in a dignified way with the meaninglessness.

So I'd just broken up with that woman, she'd gone back to her husband and children, at bottom she made a wise choice, but that made me even wearier, for I've always believed the illusion that in love a touch of madness is needed, even in fleeting love, which is easily forgotten. For we can only save another from oblivion if for a short moment they've accompanied us in some madness.

She'd left me then, and for several days I'd been wandering around the city lonely and bitter. And those were strange days, people were waiting for something, afraid of something, counting on something, dreaming of something, skeptical of something, something was driving them to self-destruction, something was holding them back, terrible days of accounts being settled between Poland and Poland, the new Poland and the old, days of reckonings which, that frosty night, were to end with the final act of subjugation, the war of the authorities with the nation, martial law.

Naturally I was mixed up in it, maybe even more than I'd have liked, because events developed rapidly, few people were in control of them; besides, at that time the opposi-

tion in Poland was not a political option but a form of con-
ditioned reflex. Whoever wanted to retain a modicum of
common sense, hold on to an ounce of independent
thought, sided with the opposition. At that time of course
no one believed that we'd succeed in bringing down communism. Communism meant the Soviet Union, and the
Soviet Union dictated its conditions to the world; it had
the world by the throat. People in Washington, Paris, and
Bonn whimpered in fear before Brezhnev and stood to attention for Soviet marshals, and in every capital of the
world at that time the Poles were looked upon as de-
sperados and troublemakers who instead of knuckling
under, sitting still and bearing their fate submissively, had
the audacity to demonstrate their anticommunism aloud
and to demand freedom, thus jeopardizing the comfort of
the West Germans, the French, and the Anglo-Saxons.

Among us, then, there was no question of bringing down
communism; to do that, if the truth be told, we'd have had
to blow up not just Moscow but also Washington, Paris,
and Bonn, and that was a task beyond even the Poles, and
so, to cut a long story short, we weren't thinking of our
own lives but only of our children and our grandchildren.
That was our most important, overriding idea, that half a
century later our grandson should not be ashamed of his
grandfather, from whose loins he had sprung forth into this
world.

As I said, at this time I was sad and embittered, for I'd been
abandoned by a nice, pretty woman, a fairly ordinary person, the kind I'd been dreaming of for years, but once I had

her in my arms, of course I felt deeply disappointed, because always, to this day, I've wanted to kill dragons for a
woman, discover new lands, cross uncharted deserts, but
her needs were less thrilling, she liked taking walks through
the city, Marszałkowska Street for instance, or Nowy
Świat, that was supposed to demonstrate her love for me.
She defied fate by walking down Nowy Świat, she played
dice with destiny, she would hold my hand, all atremble
with anxiety, instinct with that theatrical heroism of hers,
pale, yet smiling triumphantly, because at any minute she
might meet someone on the street who an hour later would
scuttle off to tell her husband, and when she came home
she would be faced with the most terrible ordeal of her life.
Betrayal, rage, jealousy, revenge, wrath, shame, in a word
the entire gamut of emotions that up till then she'd only
read about in books. But that December day, while the
thaw still lasted, for it was around midday, another woman
crossed my path.

I come out of a certain institution where some friends and I
have been plotting against the reds in fairly open fashion;
it's a quarter after twelve, Saturday, I feel somehow uneasy,
I meet a guy I know who says that he'd like to go somewhere quiet to have a good talk, he's oppressed by forebodings, he's heard some vague rumors, the army is on the
move on the highways in the direction of Warsaw, last
night someone saw great columns of tanks, have I not heard
anything, I say sure I have, there are various stories going
around, but I don't believe them, the authorities are always
trying to scare us, how many times have we heard about a

buildup of Soviet forces on the border, I think there's
method in it, don't attach any significance to that kind of
news. Nevertheless, my friend repeats obstinately that a re-
liable person saw with their own eyes formations of tanks
headed for Warsaw, someone else was stopped by an armored car, my interlocutor's very excited, I can see his eyelid fluttering nervously, he licks his chapped lips as if he
were racked by an inner fever, suddenly he says, dropping
his voice to a whisper, that his brother-in-law is in the
party, yesterday this brother-in-law was issued a handgun, a
magazine, and also written instructions saying that Solidarity is planning to murder all party members along with
their families, children included. Panic among the communists is spreading in ever-increasing circles, some of them
are demanding that they attack immediately, shoot without
mercy, they shout out at committee meetings, shoot in defense of our women, our children, where are the Soviet
divisions, why are they so late in coming to our relief?
These people are behaving as if they really were at bay, in
the meantime the city hears the ringing of church bells, people hurry from store to store to buy something to eat, everywhere there are long lines of patient, exhausted
shoppers, in these lines the communists stand shoulder to
shoulder with the anticommunists, no one wants to hurt
anyone else, those in line dream of only one thing, of reaching the counter while there's still something left to buy. I
say to my friend that that's the true barometer of moods,
but he no longer believes it, he's wiser than me by the few
hours that separate us from the truth about Poland, and
right then in the café, in the middle of our impassioned,

disjointed conversation, at the next table I notice the girl. Light blond hair, blue eyes, full lips, an exquisite oval face, a kind of shameless youth, and yet, oh my God, the girl's looking at me and smiling, a smile that's strange because it contains a promise, yet in it there's not a trace of conscious temptation. This girl is simply well disposed towards the world, she's smiling at the world, and I'm a little part of that world. I instantly lose interest in my friend's political revelations and in order to get rid of him as soon as possible I confirm his fears, I tell him in an uneasy voice that maybe we really should be afraid, heaven knows what the Soviets mean to do, I even accept those tanks on the road to Warsaw without questioning. Who knows, I say, perhaps this time the communists really are planning something awful for us, that handgun certainly makes you think, I reckon we should be prepared for the worst. Then my friend, who by now is well and truly petrified, sustained in his forebodings, finally leaves, taking with him the truth about the coming hours, and I begin to welter in a new enchantment.

Excuse me, miss, I say to the lovely blonde, don't you have the feeling that something bad's about to happen today; you give the impression of being completely calm, while from all around there's terrible news, which quite unnerves the most sober-minded people, myself for example, I envy you the calm that dwells in your heart, please, infect me with your optimism.

I speak with a certain emphasis, very animated, perturbed by the news about the tanks and the armored cars; I pass on

wholesale all the information I've just heard, I use it as a
weapon of conquest, I intensify in myself and in the girl our
eternal Polish fears, woes, and misfortunes, I have the
strange feeling that I'm virtually committing treason, but
she's so beautiful that I forgive myself everything.

In my story the tanks have already entered the city, here
and there there've been skirmishes on the streets, and my
brother-in-law, a real villain, won't part with his rifle, party
headquarters have been turned into fortresses, the girl gives
me a kindly look, in her huge, beautiful eyes there is a glimmer of irony, suddenly to my amazement and delight she
lays her hand on mine and tells me in a kindly voice to stop
this amusing monologue, I know you, she says, and I admire you greatly, we were at the meeting together yesterday, you said such wise things, it's best to remain yourself,
even if you find me attractive, which by the way is hardly
surprising, after all I'm a pretty girl, it really is best to be
yourself, you don't have to frighten me with a Soviet inter-
vention, it's enough to say that you've had a lousy day and
would like to spend a few moments with a pretty girl,
what's wrong with that, I'd be glad to have a coffee with
you, then I have to buy something to take home, you can
come with me, she says this to me, and I'm already enthralled by this girl, which is hardly surprising, this is unheard of, how did such a pretty young woman find such
wise words, such a straightforward attitude to the world, I
decide at this point, and as it soon turns out I'm right, that
she's unbearably pure-hearted, that she knows nothing of
sin, betrayal, evil, she knows nothing about the devil or
about what will happen to her that night, she's totally de-

fenseless in the face of the terrible world that is bearing down upon us this very moment.

A quarter of an hour later we're wandering around the city, a beautiful girl and an aging guy. Not an artist, a writer, statesman, or soccer player, just a regular fellow with a Warsaw address, at that time she didn't even know my name, and yet here we are together, suddenly she takes my arm. These are beautiful hours in my life, dusk is falling over Warsaw, it's getting colder, here and there street lamps are coming on, her name is Katarzyna, lovely Kasia, I call her, lovely Kasia, I say, she laughs gaily, this is more than just the whim of a beautiful girl, I don't yet know what our future will be, that future is still in the Lord God's hands, or maybe the devil's, but I know already that it's not just a whim that has brought this girl and me together, there's something strange between us, perhaps a foreboding of the disaster that's soon to befall us, perhaps a desire to rebel against the world that is around us on this day, it's enough that Kasia wants to stay with me, by my side she'll face defiantly those hours that are rumbling towards us down the dark Warsaw streets, in the ever-intensifying frost that crackles in the hardening puddles.

I remember we were together somewhere, in some crowded bar full of smoke, a babble of voices, excitement, people's faces hard, pale, proud, women looking intently into the men's eyes, the men talking indistinctly, keeping their voices down, their movements stiff, there are no conversations but only fragments of monologues, it's getting late, night has already fallen, the city's growing colder, emptier, more terrifying, I feel curiously embarrassed and at the same time elated, suddenly we're in front of the building where I was living then, the face of that lovely woman serene, still, without a word we go up the steps, I look at my watch, it's almost midnight, how time flies, I think, my Lord, I think, how am I to thank You for this gift, we get into the elevator, I live on the eighth floor, the elevator moves up slowly, I take the girl in my arms, her face is cold from the frost, I have the bizarre feeling that this isn't really happening, I'm dreaming this woman and this kiss, a long gentle kiss filled with delicacy and goodness, all of a sudden, in the elevator, in the space of a few seconds I experience a great love, and at the same time I'm seized by a dread such as I haven't known in years, the elevator climbs, at the sixth floor, I remember that exactly, kissing her eyes, I whisper, Katarzyna, my beloved Katarzyna, what's happening to us, because I sense some untruth, deception, scam, the elevator stops abruptly at the eighth floor, the girl gets out first, I follow, then I feel a knock on the back of the neck, a powerful blow with a fist, everything goes dark, then light explodes into my head once again, now I can see everything, four men are surrounding us, two plainclothes police officers and two in uniform, tall figures, unrelenting faces, they've twisted my arms behind my back, on the back of my neck I can feel the hot breath of one of my assailants, I shout furiously, What's going on, though I know what's going on, I can see our whole future, it's no longer a secret, then one of the plainclothes men says to the girl, You Solidarity whore, wait till I get between your legs, I experience a moment of the kind of hatred people die of, my heart is bursting with hatred, powerlessness, and despair, I look at the girl and I think that she must have caught a chill in that thin overcoat, this was my thought in that moment of dying, and I shout at the agent, I'll find you, you stooge, I'll find you, he hits me in the face with his fist, my clocks are going backwards by now, I can hear them, the thud of the pendulum in my chest, and so this is my world, my Poland, so what's become of thirty-five years of my life, once again I'm face to face with Longin, where is thirty-five years of the history of the world, what's happened to Poland and the Poles, where are those who were born here and died here, for there were millions of good people, where are their dreams, their ambitions, their words, deeds, curses, and virtues, what's become of that Poland, so thirty-five years have no meaning, once more I'm on the threshold, I see a dark tunnel ahead of me, I see my whole life, which has already been lived once, ahead of me, I shall have to live it again, but differently, to negate this last moment that has befallen me, and I repeat again, I'll find you, you stooge, and he hits me again with his fist, my face is streaming with blood, the agent says quietly, even politely, Say that again, and I scream furiously, I'll find you, you stooge, and I get hit in the face again, and he says, Say that again, and then I hear the girl shout, Don't say anything, don't say any more, I'm begging you, don't say anything, and for me this is like an order from the highest authority, I fall silent, full of humility and love, defiance and hatred, a weak, abused man who in one instant has been robbed of everything.

With this the tale of my strange romance does not end, but only begins.

The following seven months I spent in prison. My experiences there don't belong in this story.

She visited me regularly, taking advantage of any opportunity that presented itself. At the time I wasn't aware of how many humiliations she had to suffer to achieve this, to negotiate with the authorities for their consent for her to visit me, how many times she was insulted, degraded, ridiculed, because the regulations were unbending and severe, only wives and mothers were entitled to visit, on this question the communist authorities stood firmly in defense of holy moral principles.

But she overcame all obstacles.

Every month I was led to a small stuffy room with bars on the windows where visits took place. There she would wait for me, beautiful, grave, and indescribably gentle. I took her in my arms, she returned my embrace, stroked my face and hair with her hands, touched my lips with hers ever so slightly, though it was not a kiss but a greeting, a sign of tenderness and affection, evidence of the evangelical good that that woman brought with her.

I spent the winter in a distant prison in the far west of Poland, which could be reached only by an exceptionally grueling train ride followed by a walk of over two kilometers from the train stop along a deserted dirt track to the walls of the prison.

There were extremely heavy snows at that time, blizzards raged and there was still a severe frost; yet that girl, alone, weak, in her scanty overcoat, stumbled for hours through snowdrifts and potholes, laden with provisions for me that she'd collected day after day, taking food from her own mouth, then facing a long wait in a filthy, chilly common room, for even there they still sought to harass and humiliate her, at last we would have three-quarters of an hour to talk with each other under the vigilant, hostile eyes of the guards, and then later when I returned to my cell nearby, she would set off on the return journey, back into the blizzards and frost, through the snowdrifts to the train stop, then she'd sit in a cold, dirty, dark railway carriage virtually all through the night till she reached distant Warsaw, only to set off a month later on another terrible, lonely pilgrimage to see a stranger who had only once ever kissed her, at the wrong time, in the wrong country.

I saw her for the last time three or four days before I got out. I called her the moment I got to Warsaw. I'm here, my love, I cried, with a lump in my throat, I'm back. She replied that she was happy, and that she wished me all the best. But she didn't show up when we were supposed to meet.

She never showed up again.

Only in my dreams does she sometimes still show up.

XIV

You're very beautiful in this wind, Ruth, your hair inter-woven with the whole landscape. Though it may be that the landscape no longer exists for me, for my whole world has become immersed in you, in my crazy, painful thoughts about your thoughts, because if the truth be told I think more about your love than about you yourself. I believe what's most important to me is not you but that feeling that I've managed to wheedle out of you at the end of my wan-dering life.

That day was similar. There was also a strong wind, and the girl's hair looked like a dark cloud, like your hair now, Ruth. I remember precisely every detail, every minute, yet that's understandable, because if I ever loved any other woman before you, then it was only her, only that woman.

It may have been then that I came to the conviction that chance plays a huge role in love, that maybe it makes choices for us, determining our anxieties and our happiness. For how else can that incident be explained, the fact that it happened at that particular time, so suddenly, in pain and sorrow, on the very verge of my dreams.

You know that place, Ruth. The sky there is strange, especially as a spring dusk is drawing on. At such a time the sky deepens, as if it had risen even higher, as if God had raised the dome of the world. It's crystalline, fashioned of pale blue glass, and on this glass, as on a window pane, there lie the soft breaths of the Lord God, and they are little white clouds that float at these times high over the Grand Palais, slipping away somewhere to the right and left, towards Saint Germain des Prés or the Eiffel Tower, and in front of you, blindingly close, are the gleaming statues on the pont d'Alexandre.

It was there that I was walking then with that girl, the most beautiful girl I ever met in my life, and by then I knew too that she was the creature I'd most longed for under the sun, for whom I'd had to wait, without knowing it, through half a century of solitude, disillusionments, and failures. But maybe that was just how things were with me at that time, since I was aching, I felt abused, and my heart, torn from my breast many years before, I kept seeing against the sky, impaled upon the spire of the Eiffel Tower.

The girl and I were going to the Gare d'Orsay to see the impressionists, whom she adored with a passionate devotion, to such an extent and so openly that I actually felt envious of Manet and Renoir.

I must backtrack a few years in my story.

In that setting I'd experienced the most painful humiliation of my life. I'd rather not go into details, but you're well aware that there are women who are capable of inflicting pain on a man simply because he wasn't able or wasn't willing to accede to their demands, their expectations, their whims. That happened to me in a certain house not far from the Invalides, in a small back street where there lived a bad woman, as bad as the witches in fairy tales, one of those rarely encountered individuals who make a horror show out of their own lives. She was beautiful, chic, and had intellectual aspirations; and I think that at some time she'd been bitterly let down, someone had hurt her really badly, and so for years afterwards she'd devoted herself to sweet revenge.

I thought I'd long before forgotten about this whole business, but as it turned out I was wrong.

The girl that I'm telling you about knew nothing about my bad memories. And yet she was as sensitive as a seismograph, or perhaps not so much sensitive as good and compassionate towards me, as we were passing the Grand Palais she stopped all of a sudden and, touching my arm, said it'd be better if we just went back to the Rond Point now.

But I wanted to go on, towards that bad place. She stood on the sidewalk and took me by the arm in the kind of devoted and tender gesture that bespeaks true affection.

It's a funny thing with women, I mean young women, that they have no difficulty lying with words or with looks, but their hands and arms usually tell the truth. She said then that it wouldn't be good, that she'd had second thoughts, she didn't feel like the impressionists any more. But I was determined to go on. I thought that if anyone was going to save me from those memories, it could only be her, with her I should gaze upon that building and utter in silence the curse that would liberate me. We crossed the bridge. The river was slightly ruffled, a gentle breeze was blowing, there wasn't a cloud in the sky, for a moment I even had the impression that we were alone in the city, I couldn't hear the din from the street or see the crowds of tourists heading towards the Invalides.

And suddenly something strange happened to me; maybe it was a dream that had been haunting me for years, maybe the memory of some forgotten truth that returns at certain moments of one's life, in any case the whole scene changed all at once, I was no longer on the bridge, I now saw not the Invalides but an orchard outside a house, and the house was illuminated by the rising sun in a cold gray sky, the orchard was surrounded by a luxuriant green hedge, beyond lay fallow fields, mysterious somehow and alien as often happens in dreams, when you know that something is familiar and yet unfamiliar, you sense that it is your world and yet not entirely yours, woods extended across the horizon, and from the woods a rider was galloping towards me on a foam-flecked bay gelding, it was the gelding that linked me most firmly to the real world, because I used to ride a horse like that in the early years of my life, during the war, as a young boy, at the house of a family friend, that horse was a powerful bay gelding that I loved dearly, I used to gallop bareback on it, a joyful, suntanned kid, unaware of what the future held in store for him, and it was then, as I crossed the bridge with the wonderful woman whom I loved and the dome of the Invalides vanished from my sight, that the horse appeared on the horizon all covered in foam, thundering at a gallop straight at the hedge behind which I stood in the garden; it bore someone on its back, it was me yet it was not me, someone else in my skin, I've never told you about him and I never will, everyone has such a corner in his heart where he hides his other world, inaccessible to others, where there are attics, maybe even sometimes drawing rooms, various characters walk about there, from reality and from dreams, different objects have been gathered there that existed in real life or maybe only in the imagination, a whole big world known only to God and to the devil, who look in from time to time, and at those times the person shouts out at night in their sleep, or in the middle of the street, in a crowd, clutches at their heart, seized with a terrible pain that no one else is capable of understanding, and so I was galloping from over there, or someone who was a part of me was galloping on that gelding, it was a bizarre moment since I could still feel on my arm the delicate touch of the woman's hand, and through a haze I could see the dome of the Invalides, I could hear the buzz of human voices, the noisy German and American tourists of whom there are so many in Paris, and I could also see before me the rider on the foam-flecked horse, he was dressed in a costume that I had always dreamed of as a child, that was how the members of the Committee for Public Safety dressed, those were the clothes that Saint-Just once wore, the rider had on a crimson frock coat, trousers tucked into his stockings, elkhide shoes, he looked elegant, his face was weary and stamped with an evil beauty, a huge man, I won't tell you his name, though I know it, let that name be hidden forever and forever cursed, and when the horse reared up at the hedge, abruptly reined in, when the foam dripped from its nostrils onto the freshly mown grass, at that moment the girl gave a piercing cry, for a moment I saw the dome of the Invalides, the girl called almost in despair, Please, I beg you, I want to go back to the other side, but I answered calmly, It won't take a minute, I have something to take care of here, it sounded like a madman's voice, for I was in that madness of mine, right then, at the same time, the huge man jumped down nimbly from the saddle onto the grass, he came up to me, suddenly there was no hedge, we were standing face to face, me and him in front of me, me and me in front of me, he reached out his arm, he wore a gauntlet on his hand, he touched my breast, he sunk his fingers deep into it and pulled out my heart, he threw it behind him contemptuously, he said something very quietly, I'll never tell you what he said to me, it was something immeasurably important, everyone at least once in his life hears words like these, which he should keep to himself till he dies, he can entrust them only to God at the hour of judgment, he said those words to me then, as the horse snorted behind him, I could smell horse sweat, the grass that had been mowed the day before at dusk, the exhaust fumes from the cars on the bridge, the scent of that beautiful girl's hair, it was your hair, Ruth, but I also smelled something alien, strange and mysterious, maybe it was the snuff that the rider took, or maybe it was sulfur from hell, because he was undoubtedly all steeped in it, after all it was from there that he'd come to me, we were both from there, the girl gripped my arm, it was a terrible moment, on the one hand redemption, the love of a woman so beautiful and so longed for, on the other hand a mass of figures who had gathered behind the rider, people in striped uniforms, with wooden clogs on their bare feet, like the fishermen in the Dutch old masters, their faces empty and expressionless, for where there is too much suffering there is no more emotion, the face of Christ at the moment of His dying was so exhausted as to be almost bland, they looked the same, many faces, my own faces, against this background the rider with the evil eyes, yet they were my eyes, Ruth, because everyone has moments of such looks, and then, in this crowd of downtrodden people, with shaved heads, inhuman faces, eyes blinded with suffering, emaciated limbs, in the stench of misery, of blood coagulating on fresh wounds, the sweat of death, amid curses and groans, in those bizarre sounds of a world where the crack of the lash and the sizzle of burning bodies are interwoven with Mozart and Bach, and the rustle of ashes falling on the grate seems louder than the singing of a pious Christian, Jew, and mullah together calling upon God to be a witness to human destiny, at that very moment the rider handed me an official document with a seal and ordered me to read it. It was a death sentence brought against someone. That person's head was to fall right at that moment, at dawn, at sunrise, on the Paris scaffold.

I leaned against the balustrade, I looked at the waters of the river, on them the glittering light shimmered, then the girl said, I won't be able to love you if we go on, because we're crossing to the other side against my wishes, that was what she said then, and I suddenly felt that I'd at last been released, for the first time in my life I had the feeling that there was someone who thought about me more frequently and more passionately than about herself.

We returned to the hotel. The whole way back she held my arm, as if afraid that I'd run away again to some hell. And in the hotel room, from the window of which you could see the outline of the Défense, those tall, tapering, cylindrical signs of the next century, which will come to give people once more a ray of hope and a handful of illusions, in that hotel room, where pop music could be heard next door, and farther away, somewhere in the depths of the immense city there were prayers and singing, conversations and curses, right there she took me in her arms and loved me like no other woman ever loved me in my life.

She saved me.

She is in me, Ruth. You are her, Ruth.

XV

He stood on the terrace, in the thick mist. Yet the grass in the garden looked very fresh. Farther off the lamps shone over the swimming pool. In their light women in swimsuits moved about. They were slim and shapely, and they wore colored caps on their heads. The first expedition from Mars, which has come specially to the Glesses' to attend their reception, Kamil thought maliciously.

He went into the drawing room, and passed among the guests who had gathered. They stared at him curiously; someone said aloud:

"That's him."

Someone else added more quietly:

"He's recording his story."

Suddenly Ruth drew near.

"Have my legs gone? Maybe I've drunk too much," said Kamil.

"Your legs are still there," she replied, and laughed. She had a beautiful laugh, and even more beautiful dark, elongated eyes.

"But I think my head is missing," he said. "It's Mr. Gless's whiskey. Or perhaps the climate here. Or something else that I can't pinpoint. A sense of falsehood. I don't belong here, Ruth."

She looked at him closely, and all at once in her elongated eyes he saw a trace of weariness. God, he thought in a sudden panic, if she's had enough of me, where will I go in this world? Paying no attention to where they were, he seized Ruth's hand and kissed it.

She laughed freely, but that trace remained in her eyes.

"I'm beginning to be afraid," he said.

"Of what?"

"Of you losing patience. I mean well, Ruth. I've never been a burden for a woman. Everything is different than I would have wished."

"I'm not losing patience at all," she responded. "You're the one who's always in a hurry. Now why don't you go back to the terrace. There are a number of nice people up there. You could have a chat with them."

"I could, but being advised to chat with a guy who makes artificial chickens' eggs sounds killing. It's like suggesting to a man who's swimming to a life raft from a sinking ship that he should cook himself a steak, because it's a good idea to eat something hot before he sinks to the bottom of the sea."

"Go eat something hot," she said with a smile, and left him.

The lawn was soft and damp. The Chinese lanterns cast colored patches of light. Kamil felt his head spinning in a hollow, painful way. Why should this happen to me, he thought, I've known how to drink for years, these people here are children compared to me, so why is this happening to me? All at once he recalled a strange story. It may have been a dream remembered, and it may not have been.

He thought that back then the black guy must have hidden behind the caryatid; there was no other way down, only the stairs, the caryatid on the landing, the window set farther in, through which blew a damp wind smelling of smog. The black man was coming slowly down the stairs. A heavy man's footsteps. All of a sudden he disappeared. The plainclothes officer at the precinct had said: "You were lucky. Someone was there at that time."

I don't remember, thought Kamil, I don't remember. In the car. At the side of the highway. She was stunningly beautiful. The trucks rumbling along. A thick mist. He said to her: "You were never so beautiful as that afternoon, in the car, on the hard shoulder of the highway, as the trucks were rumbling along through the mist. They were rumbling along, sneaking past, in the mist." She said suddenly: "That's not what I wanted. It was a mistake. Now everything will be different, and I'll never be free again."

Someone was coming up from the direction of the swimming pool. Tall, slim, in a tuxedo. As he passed Kamil he sneered loudly and distinctly:

"Hi there, shortass."

"Give it a rest, Schubert," Kamil retorted quietly, looking around uneasily. "Those days are long gone. I don't give a damn about you. You simply don't exist. But if you want to talk with me, let's meet in Zurich. I can even go tomorrow. Let's meet."

"That can be arranged, shortass," replied the man in the tuxedo.

Suddenly Kamil staggered and leaned on the door that led from the terrace to the drawing room. Someone behind him asked quietly and politely:

"Are you all right?"

"I'm fine," replied Kamil.

Gless showed up. His face wore a grudging expression. They stood facing each other and Gless touched Kamil's arm lightly with his open hand.

"You're not feeling tired?" he asked.

"No," answered Kamil.

"Pity," said Gless. "Because I've got a car to take you back to the hotel."

"You're very kind, Mr. Gless," said Kamil.

They both set off in silence towards the parking lot. It was darker there. Gless suddenly seemed to relax; his voice sounded amicable:

"When are you returning to Warsaw?" he asked.

"It doesn't depend on me. We're making these recordings."

"So I've heard. Apparently they're interesting. But you must be finishing now."

"It depends on Mrs. Gless," said Kamil.

"Not only on her," said Gless. "In three days I leave for the States. I'm planning to take my wife with me."

"That would indicate that we'll have to finish," said Kamil calmly. His heart ached.

They were standing by the car. Gless offered his hand and said:

"I doubt we shall see each other again. I wish you a safe trip home."

Kamil got in the car. It moved off.

Gless, thought Kamil, I assure you that you won't be able to handle me. Better men than you have failed to.

He laughed quietly. After a moment he said to the driver:

"What's this town called?"

"Baiser," replied the driver.

"Sounds nice," said Kamil. "Do you know who Beria was?"

"Beria?" repeated the driver, drawing the name out. "Never heard of him."

"You're a lucky man," said Kamil. "Baiser. Really nice."

The hotel foyer was deserted and quiet. The doorman, seeing Kamil, said with a polite, artificial smile:

"Bonne nuit, monsieur."

Then the elevator. Moving up without a sound. Electronic key. Door. Room. The wind was making the curtains billow out. Like the time he was with her. She wore a crimson blouse and close-fitting jeans.

He went up to her, put his arms around her.

"No," she said. "I don't like to be touched. Please, don't touch me."

He said rather sharply:

"Have you gone mad? There are only two rational explanations for such behavior, Irena."

She sat in an armchair and looked at him with something of a sneer.

"Only two?" she drawled. "I wonder what they might be."

"Either you've suddenly begun to find me repellent, or else this is some vile game," he replied.

"And if I find you repellent? What then?"

He answered that that doesn't happen from one day to the next.

"Nothing's occurred since yesterday. So tell me, who was here?"

"No one was here," she said. "You're imagining things again."

"When I tried to kiss you three days ago," he said, "you asked me not to. You had it your way. I said that if such is your whim, then of course I give in. No, you replied, it's your high-mindedness, you're just wise and you know what to do . . ."

He went up to the window and drew aside the curtain. The water down below was calm, cars were crossing the bridge, the neon lights were on as usual.

"I'm going to bed," he muttered aloud. "I'll have one brandy then I'm going to bed. But all the same you won't leave, Gless. Or you'll leave alone. This time I'm not going to surrender. Enough of this high-mindedness."

He took off his jacket and sat in the armchair. I'd like to die, he thought. Nothing's going to come of this. I've missed my chance. All these years I never knew how. Now it's too late.

Baiser, he thought, how nice that sounds. That Schubert pops up everywhere. Even in such good, refined, completely innocent company.

On the boulevard microscopic droplets of moisture

settled on his face. Then the pleasant, somewhat soporific smell of the taxi. Baiser, he repeated to himself, I expect some poet thought it up. The house was dark. As he crossed the lawn he could hear splashes from the pool. Who was still bathing at this hour?

Suddenly a dog barked.

Like that time, in the night. A very thick mist. Reiner had two dogs. One was called Nero, the other Wolf. Nero was old, he could be reasoned with. Nero, I called, Nero, don't be a bad boy. I think he understood a bit. He would just tug at my trouser leg.

The dog barked again.

Nero, it's me, do you remember me?

But it wasn't Nero, it was Wolf, who would always leap at your throat. Without warning. Somewhere close by, in the darkness, Reiner was hiding. His sweating face shone in the dark like the moon behind clouds. The crack of a whip in the air. Wherever Reiner goes, his whip goes with him. Wherever the whip goes, the crack goes with it.

The door was ajar. He went into the drawing room. The furniture stood lifeless, covered with white-and-blue-striped dustsheets, like Jewish paschal frontals. So they're going to America after all. In two or three days.

Wolf came in. He was a Doberman with a long dry snout. His eyes gleamed green in the dark of the drawing room. Wolf, it's me, leave me alone, I don't have any business with your Reiner, he's not the one who's going to hang.

The dog gave a whine, turned around sluggishly, and lay down on the rug.

A wall clock struck somewhere.

Am I here? It's too late for anything. Nothing will come of it. I've missed my chance. When did I miss it? Why? Nothing will come of it. They put the covers on the furniture as soon as the last guests had left. She didn't say a word. She's running away from me. Disgust.

He walked upstairs. The carpet deadened his footsteps. There was a smell of oranges. They're leaving for Veracruz. To go and be compassionate. You don't have to travel so far to do that. Where does he sleep, that manufacturer of artificial eggs?

Baiser, how beautiful.

Gless stood before him in a tuxedo; an untied black bow tie lay loose on his shirt front.

"What are you doing here?" asked Gless. "Why did you bring the dog in? I don't allow the dogs in the living room."

"Wolf," called Kamil. "Attack."

Wolf was not there.

Ruth suddenly appeared. She was wearing a thin brown overcoat and a dark woollen cap that covered her magnificent, luxuriant hair.

"Ruth," cried Kamil, "why are you wearing eyeglasses?"

"I'm shortsighted," she replied.

"She has bad eyesight," said Gless sharply. "Her eyesight is getting worse, that awful wife of mine."

All at once he raised his arm and struck Ruth in the face, knocking her glasses to the floor.

A piercing noise rang out, and Kamil screamed at the top of his voice:

"Gless, I'll have to kill you now!"

They both fell down the stairs, but Reiner grabbed Kamil by the shoulders and said politely:

"I still need you for dying."

Ruth was weeping bitterly and repeating that Kamil must trust her.

"I have nothing to hide," she said, "nothing to hide. You're in my house. You can look in all the nooks and crannies. There's nothing here against you."

"This isn't your home," he retorted with a feeling of impotent despair. "The real one you're hiding from me. I've never suffered so much as from the fact that I'm not allowed into your home. For this reason you have no right to talk of love, Ruth. Nothing has ever made me suffer so much in my life."

Someone knocked at the door. Kamil rose from the armchair and staggered towards the wall.

"Is everything all right?" asked a voice at the door. "Do you need help with anything?"

"No," he replied. "Thank you."

Silence. He returned to the armchair. He thought he must be drunk. But he was slowly sobering up. He could tell from a different kind of pain. He was slowly sobering up in order to move step by step closer to that worst, most devastating fear, the compelling thought that he was being deceived. But she isn't lying, he told himself, she's honest and she isn't lying. Yet he knew that lying is not the only kind of deception. It can also take the form of stubborn silence.

My God, he was saying to himself, staring at the cur-

tain billowing out from the open window like the sail of a
yacht gliding soundlessly along, driven by a gentle breeze,
past the wooded shores of Wigry Lake, my God, he
thought, and he was happy to be sailing along alone and
terrified that lies would drown him momentarily, my God,
why do You allow a woman to have so many secrets? Who
did I love there, in that ghastly city, built from ruins on the
crushed bones of thousands of innocent victims, and who
do I love here, amidst the mountains and lakes of this Swiss
innocence? What does it come down to, my knowledge of
the woman for whom I'm prepared to die in disquiet and
torment? I don't know a single day of her past, not a single
thought of hers about the world, I know none of her sufferings and none of her joys, her fears, her hopes, or her
dreams, I don't know the evil that dwells in her or the good
with which she has been endowed, I don't know anything
about her, because when I ask she's silent, when I speak
she's silent, when I beg she's silent, when I call she's silent,
when I suffer she's silent, and I know only her beautiful
elongated eyes, her mysterious smile, the touch of her
hand, and maybe too that hour of her life that she is giving
fleetingly to me.

I've missed my chance, he thought, staring at the sail
of the curtain, which was allowing him to travel far away
from this hotel room, in the dusk falling over Wigry Lake,
in the woods, where somewhere, years ago, he had experienced the truth about the world, without a woman and
without love, where he had often heard the step of the elk
heading down to the water's edge to drink slowly and
proudly, where he saw the silvery scales of pike thrashing

about in nets drawn in towards the shoreline with its under-
growth full of grebes rising into a straight, startled flight
over the tops of the pine trees, where beneath the clouds
the hawk circles, slow and watchful, seeking out hares from
high above, where everything he saw and heard was a simple truth of life, without imaginings or lies, disguises or illusions, without that whole shame of ignorance that had now
fallen to his lot.

I missed my chance, he thought.

Then he rose, went to the window, drew aside the curtain, looked at the foreign street of the foreign city, swathed
in darkness and mist, and recited in a whisper the litany of
desperate lostness.

XVI

"What's she like?" Ruth asked suddenly.

They were sitting on the terrace of a small café; cars were passing on the boulevard, moving with a certain stateliness, looking a little unreal against the background of the waters of the lake, somewhere far off bells were ringing sonorously, and Kamil thought worriedly that perhaps this is feeding time for the Calvinist angels, who fly in to Geneva to partake of divine provender. Along the sidewalk, walking slowly, came a very black man in a long, stylish overcoat that reached almost to the ground; he wore a yellow foulard scarf around his neck that flowed casually from his shoulders, he looked at Ruth brazenly, only blacks and Poles look at women like that, no one else is bold enough. Ruth put her hand on Kamil's; Kamil raised his eyes, filled with anxiety, gratitude, and pain, and said:

"Who, Ruth?"

"Your wife," she answered.

He laughed with relief:

"That's really odd. After all you've heard about me up

till now, can you really think I've ever had a wife? I've never had a wife. Only a strong man can marry."

"Only a strong man," she repeated thoughtfully, pursing her lips slightly.

The black man was coming back along the sidewalk; he dragged his leg as if he had suddenly become lame. The yellow scarf hung down below his knees.

"Do you ever organize hunts for them?" asked Kamil. "In our country I think that would catch on. So that's how it is. There was a time I wanted to get married. It was one of the few women I didn't love. And there was no one else involved. A very good-looking brunette, dark-skinned, striking, a Creole kind of beauty. She was the right person for a wife. She had the potential for making an entrance, if you know what I mean by that. For Gless you make the best entrances in the whole of Europe north of the Alps. It's a pity you can't see his expression at such times. But I've seen him."

Ruth frowned.

"There's not much I can offer him," she said. "It's sad."

"He's a happy man," said Kamil. "Don't reproach yourself, he's happier than he deserves."

Ruth's face took on an expression of concentration. Her eyes seemed anxious.

"What do you mean?" she asked. "Have you been talking to my husband?"

"A few words," replied Kamil. "Of no significance. He said he's going to America. And he wished me a safe trip home."

"I didn't know he was going to the States again," said Ruth. "When did he tell you this?"

"At the party."

"I'm a little taken aback," she said.

Then Kamil said angrily:

"How long is all this going to last?"

"I don't see any reason why it shouldn't just last."

The black man came into the café; his scarf brushed against the tables. His eyes were bloodshot, he was unshaven, and he gave off the smell of a strong eau de toilette.

"He's coming back from seeing a woman," said Kamil suddenly.

"How do you know?" asked Ruth.

"A quarter of an hour ago he was with a woman," said Kamil. His voice shook with an inner tension. "He was with her for several hours."

"How do you know?" repeated Ruth.

"I know," he replied, and looked her in the eye, terrified.

Then for a long time he sat without moving, listening to his strange voices.

"My heart aches," he said finally.

"What does that mean?" she asked.

"My heart aches," he repeated. "I'm old, tired, spent, and my heart aches because it's toiled hard in this life, in various situations it's had too much to bear, and now it simply aches."

"I don't want that," said Ruth. "We'll go and see Fischer right away."

"Who's Fischer?" asked Kamil.

"My doctor," she answered. She seemed worried, her movements became less fluid, her eyes watched Kamil with that trace of anxiety that always moved him in every woman in the world.

"Ruth," he said. "It's a different kind of ache."

"What do you mean?"

"It aches from unhappiness, it's a kind of Polish heart-ache, it's only found in Poland, it's probably because of our climate, but medically speaking it's not serious, though of course you can die from it, but you can always die."

"You frightened me," she came back. "I don't like that way of talking."

"It's starting," said Kamil, completely calm now. "It's starting, what you don't like about me, what displeases you in me, all my best, my most admirable traits will be precisely those that you won't be able to stand; so it's starting, after only a few days, and you say that we can last forever."

"I accept you," she said softly. "I know there are different worlds, even God is probably not the same here as in Warsaw, I accept that, there are certain things I don't like, I'm entitled to that, but that doesn't mean you have to change for me. My Lord, what right do I have to make any demands?"

"You have every right," said Kamil. "No one before you had any. But that's where the whole problem lies."

It occurred to him that in fact she already had everything he could give her. That's the whole point, he thought, that she has too much. And there's not enough of me left for myself. It was never like this before. No one before had rights to me, no one managed to force them on me. Could

Hitler have dreamed of having rights to me like this? Actually, I was able quite easily, without particularly trying, to protect from him my right to be myself, his frenzied efforts came to nothing, they were to no avail, he could grind me to a powder, bury me a hundred meters underground, he could gas me and burn me, but he didn't have me even for a moment, because I was always myself, perhaps more myself than at any time later, for the other one employed better methods, he was more complex. When it came down to it Hitler affected only my body, my legs, arms, shoulders, they shaved my head, dressed me in a clownish uniform with blue and white stripes, ordered me to feed out of a bowl like a dog, I had to do exercises across a thousand miles of assembly ground, I had to watch as they hanged some poor soul from the gallows, but what more could they do to me? It was only a matter of the body, the staying power of the muscles, bones, joints. The other one, however, had rather different methods, he acted more ingeniously, he didn't just kill but also posed certain questions, for instance about the limits of freedom, about equality and justice, and who doesn't hunger after justice, who is free from that yearning? He knew what he was doing, he operated differently, in one sense there was even something alluring in it, a new solution to problems that in the end always turn out to be insoluble, yet the longing remains, a beautiful yearning, maybe even at such times there stirs within you a fleeting memory of paradise, our longing for utopia. He achieved a certain success in this, better people than I yielded, they were blind, deaf, and dumb in the face of tyranny, so with Stalin I had without doubt a more difficult time, but I managed, I lost nothing of myself, maybe he just taught me dissimulation, acquainted me with the evil that dwells in people, which at bottom means getting to know oneself, yet I retained my individuality, I had my secrets, I was full of puzzles that the world could not solve, and now nothing is left, she has all of me in that small, slender hand of hers, and I no longer exist apart from her, I no longer exist without her. Where are those sacred mysteries of mine, where are the trunks full of my adventures, with all those Indian headdresses at the bottom, those huge, wonderful trunks that I could never get closed because they were so full of bodies, and finally where am I, if not in the last hiding place left to me, that tiny little boat of her eyes, which is sailing to destruction.

So once again I've picked the wrong card, and wherever I go I'm faced with the same test, which I cannot pass.

Jezebel, I can see you still, I can always see you, you're wearing close-fitting jeans, a crimson blouse, your ash-blond hair fastened at the back with a barrette, tall, slim, deceitful and godless Jezebel, I hate you, you didn't deserve any better.

I killed her. I killed her? Ruth, did I kill her?

A breeze began to blow from the lake and it suddenly became a little cooler, though the sun was still hot, the sky was deep blue like in Warsaw sometimes, in October, when the early frosts come at daybreak in the Łazienki Gardens, the yellow leaves on the pathways give out a strange metallic crunch underfoot, here and there squirrels are scurrying about, on all the paths the split shells of the chestnuts are turning black, and over the immense trees stretches the glassy silver and blue sky like a window pane that separates the city from a longed-for redemption.

It will end sooner or later, thought Kamil, and he was immediately seized with terror. He saw before him the dark tunnel of return, all those people, the living and the dead, and the streets, the squares and marketplaces, on them the stumps of burnt trees, smoke from fires that never went out, ashes that never cooled, yet he knew that there was no other way out. It must end, how long can one pretend that a person does not have a real life.

I've lost my mind, thought Kamil, I must draw in the reins, I'll leave, I'll leave tomorrow. He looked at Ruth. I'll leave in two days, in three, he thought.

"I think I'll be leaving in a week," he said.

"You don't have to," she replied. "You said yourself that you don't have anywhere to go back to."

"Where am I supposed to stay? It's a bit pathetic. All of a sudden I've become homeless. I can't be so frivolous. I mean, at my age you don't start over with everything from the beginning."

"It's always possible to start over," said Ruth. "You know that better than I do."

"And you," said Kamil, "would you be prepared to start over with everything?"

"That's exactly what I'm doing," she said, and burst out laughing. "Is something more needed? I think it's possible to be contented with what there is."

"And what is there?" he asked aggressively. "What is there, can you tell me that?"

"A little love," she answered unruffled. "That's a great deal."

But he wouldn't listen to this. Now he was hearing the dull thud of a gate being slammed, the clatter of rolling stones, the rattle of tiles falling from a height.

"There's something that we can't name with this stunted language of ours," he said very calmly, quietly, gently. "There's a rift between you and me, between this boulevard and the street I live on in Warsaw, between the glass in front of me and the glass in my apartment, there's a rift between our acts and our thoughts, and maybe something more, Ruth, something that is never mentioned because it doesn't have a name and never did, but I know there's a deep rift between us, or simply the Red Sea, which we shall be unable to cross, because it won't ever part, this time there won't be any Moses, God has condemned us to be different, and whoever rejects this will lose his self. I'm not just talking about my Polishness, because it's not so difficult to get rid of that, but about the life-curse that I carry about with me everywhere I go. Long into the night I'm unable to get to sleep, my room is full of demons. I don't want them to be clamoring over your head, Ruth. Let me tell you something important. I belong to the accursed tribe whom the world never liked, for those like me it was always a crowded, dark place devoid of prospects. I'm from the tribe of those who were born to live and die in suffering, perhaps that's why I'm Polish, I think it may have been God's intention to make all those tormented, feckless, miserable, and yet also somewhat base and foolish people Poles, to gather them all in one place, on the Vistula, on those banks that never begin and never end, birches, willows, the whole world flat and shallow like the bottom of a casket. That's where I'm from, Ruth, and that's where I belong."

"Nonsense," said Ruth. "Nonsense."

"Don't talk to me like that," said Kamil angrily.

Yet he suddenly seized her hand, and when she tried to close it he kissed the palm roughly and said in despair:

"Save me, Ruth."

"I can't do it alone," she replied.

"Yes," he said, "of course."

Then he was silent for a long time, and Ruth stroked his hand tenderly as it lay motionless on the table, as if it had been cut off.

"I had a dream," he said finally.

"What dream? Surely you don't believe in dreams?"

He laughed harshly.

"That black man has just come back from seeing a woman," he said.

"What's that got to do with it?" she asked, looking inside the café. Against the wall sat the black man with the bloodshot eyes, in the yellow scarf that hung down almost to the ground. He sat morosely, absorbed in himself, sipping a citron pressé.

"He's just come back from seeing a woman," repeated Kamil with a pitiless obstinacy. "I'll prove it to you."

"How? What do you mean to do? This is nonsense."

"Don't talk like that to me, I've asked you already," he said. "And what does 'nonsense' mean anyway? Maybe it's something that was not dreamt of in your philosophy; but I dreamt of it once, even though I'm a mere plaything of destiny."

All of a sudden he smoothed out a paper napkin on the table top and took out a pen.

"What is it?" asked Ruth.

Kamil wrote a few words on the napkin, beckoned the waiter, and told him to give the napkin to the black man.

"What are you playing at?" said Ruth. "Why are you doing this?"

The black man read the napkin, looked up in surprise, then transferred his gaze to Kamil, nodded, and stood up; the scarf slipped down his body and gently slid towards the floor. The man came up, cocked his head slightly like a bird about to fly off from a tree, and said softly:

"You know her?"

"No," replied Kamil.

"So what does this mean?" asked the man. "And why?"

"I don't know her," said Kamil. "I don't know anything about her."

"So why the note?" asked the man.

"I don't know," said Kamil. "It's about a woman."

"Sure," answered the man. "But you say you don't know her."

"It's not about her," said Kamil.

"Who's it about?" asked the man.

"About her," said Kamil, and touched Ruth's hand.

"Who are you?" the black man asked Ruth. A milder tone had entered his voice; his scarf slipped slightly. He straightened it on his shoulders with the unconscious yet studied gesture with which beautiful women straighten their hair. The man's eyes began to shine, his large, deep brown lips moved delicately as if they were relishing the air that rose over Ruth's head.

"I'm sorry," said Ruth. "This is just some nonsense. He has a weak heart."

"You shouldn't feel sympathy for anyone," said the man. "No one in this world deserves it. I mean it. So who are you?"

"Just tell me whether the address is right," said Ruth.

"Yes," confirmed the man. "That's why I'm talking to you."

"It's a coincidence," said Ruth. "I'm really sorry about all this."

The man moved his lips again; they parted, so that his white teeth could be seen, he now looked like a cannibal or a famous prophet, or a famous gangster, he'd suddenly acquired some kind of stateliness and foreignness. He said:

"That can't be. It shouldn't be. Let him explain."

"And if he can't?" asked Ruth, and concern and anxiety could be heard in her voice.

"Why can't he?" said the black man.

They were talking about Kamil as if he were dead, or had gone out for a walk, or as if they'd forgotten about him. Ruth looked straight into the black man's eyes, the black man looked into her eyes, they had known each other for a long time, they may even have shared a life together, Kamil felt abandoned and betrayed, he thought that this is the start, at last something is beginning, abandonment and a terrible loneliness have cleared the way to the place he had long been heading for, on the other side there would be resolution, all he had to do was to get through. On the other side would be resolution.

Suddenly the black man sat down at the table and

leaned over towards Ruth; they looked into each other's eyes, and she said gently, almost tenderly:

"He had a dream. He says it's from the dream."

"Yes," said the man. "I think that explains a lot."

"Why?" asked Ruth. "A dream?"

"A dream," said the man. "I have dreams too. Do you have dreams?"

"No," replied Ruth. "And even if I do, they have no meaning for me."

"They may have meaning for others," said the man.

"That's terrifying," said Ruth.

"He's not from here," the black man said with such certainty in his voice that it was as if he too had had a dream and so knew a great deal about Kamil. "He's from far away. Like I'm from far away. That's how he's able to know something. You can't, but he can. But I don't think he'll say any more. Strange. A great pity. If I were him I'd say a lot more. But he won't say any more because he hates black people."

"Nonsense," said Ruth.

"Don't talk like that," said the black man, a little angrily. "Say you don't understand. 'I don't understand,' say that. Don't ever say it differently."

"Okay," she said. "So I'm saying that I don't understand."

"Not everyone understands," replied the man. "And that's how it should be. It's better that way."

He fell silent for a moment, studying Ruth. Then he looked at Kamil. Turning back to Ruth, he asked:

"Is he in pain?"

"I'm not in pain now," replied Kamil. "And I don't

know any more. If I did it would be a different matter. I'd say. But I only know the address."

"Don't go there, man," the black man said mildly. "It's not a good place for us. It's not a good place for anyone."

He stood up from the table; the scarf slipped down, brushing against the floor.

"Maybe someone's died, eh? Maybe someone's passed away?" asked the man, looking intently into Kamil's eyes. He was speaking more quietly now; his voice had become strangely hoarse.

"I don't know," said Kamil. "That's precisely the point, I don't know."

Ruth cried out. The waiter appeared. Small, brisk, gray-haired, polite.

"Have you spilt something, perhaps, ma'am?"

"No," said Ruth. "Nothing's happened."

The waiter bowed and left. The black man nodded.

"Sometimes it's better to spill something," he said. "That way there's some kind of order in a person."

He stood for a moment in silence. He looked at Ruth. Perhaps with a touch of sympathy. All at once he set off towards the exit. Behind him, along the ground he dragged the scarf, yellow as daffodils.

"I don't understand," said Ruth. "Is it here that love ends?"

XVII

It's hard for me to put into words how much our closeness helps me. There are things I couldn't talk about in the studio, in the presence of Jean Claude and the others, even though I know that tomorrow, or in a month's time, large numbers of strangers will be listening to my confessions anyway.

But the process itself of formulating one's thoughts, of summoning oneself from memory, wrestling with a memory that is crippled, like someone whose leg has been torn off in a traffic accident, this is a tough business; you alone know how much our conversations cost me, and that's why I need you so much now, you, your looks, your gestures, your touch.

Ruth, in a way I'm preparing for death, don't you think?

There come to me the shades either of the dead or of something even worse. There come to me my own demons, whom I had put to sleep in the deepest, darkest prisons, in my Schlüsselburg castles, in my Moabits, and I entertained a fool's blind hope that they would never find me again. But they're at my side once more, dictating my thoughts and words, pulling me back into the vortex I escaped from not long ago so as to live a little more like a human being.

But maybe I'm destined never to be freed, always to dwell in the meaninglessness of that world. Maybe people like me are needed to carry that world across to the farther, better shore. As a warning? As a reminder? As a memorial to undying stupidity in suffering?

It's good that you're with me. It's good that there is this room. It's good that there is this city. Everything is good. Even my memory may turn out to be good, for there is a trace of good in it, don't you think? After all, I remembered only such a world as I wished to conserve. It's better than the real one. Because I believe I'm better than the world I was given to live in.

Ruth, my love, the past fortunately doesn't exist, it's not there, there's only the remembered world, the one we preserve in ourselves. And this changes along with us. That is good; it's the best thing man was given by nature. That his past grows with him. And dies with him.

Okay, Ruth. We can start recording, my lovely. I'll tell you about a woman I loved dearly and unhappily, because she couldn't meet me halfway at the right time. My friends told me I had to go to Radom. When you look at the world from the windows of this hotel, cities like Radom have no right whatsoever to exist. Yet they do exist. At that time it was a dirty, crowded, run-down city full of weary people devoid of hope. Big industrial plants, various types of manufacturing, an important working-class center.

One day Radom couldn't take it any more. Cities behave like people, who put up patiently with adversity, in humility of spirit, until in the end there comes a moment of crisis, when a person can't take it for a second longer, the world has him by the throat, he's filled with despair but there's no room in him for that despair, it's drowning him without any hope of rescue, at such times the person's thoughts and feelings are in chaos, he may even realize that shouting or crying won't change anything, or it'll even make the present situation worse, but he's lost control over himself and he blows up. That happens sometimes with a humiliated, degraded, enslaved city. People can no longer walk about the streets, every word and gesture incline them to rebellion, to shouting out; and finally comes the great moment of purging. Then no one thinks that tomorrow or the next day things will get better, because no one thinks at all about tomorrow or the next day.

Ruth, cities too have their bad dreams. It's not only in the middle of the night that you have to fight with demons. You have to face them in the bright light of day.

Those were times when the foolish communist authorities had become prey to certain delusions regarding their popularity. For a few years life in Poland really had been better, the country was becoming more civilized, because the government had adopted an audacious, risky policy of taking out loans, they had their shortsighted allies in the west, the dollars were flooding in, these were supposed to be wise long-term investments, but the government, desperate for approval, allowed the money to be spent on consumables, they even encouraged it, and indeed in the space of a few years there was a significant improvement, and the mood seemed better than ever before. But there soon came a slump; a deep crisis set in, inflation, shortages of goods, people were more and more discontented, there was more and more bitterness, the country was once again in the grip of a massive scam, and the authorities, feverishly seeking a stop-gap solution, raised food prices drastically: It was then that Radom couldn't take it any longer.

The whole city came to a standstill, the strike affected almost all the big plants, thousands of desperate people crowded out into the streets.

The authorities proved to be very shrewd and very brazen. True, they revoked the price rises for fear of a broader wave of strikes across the whole country, but the city was dealt with in a horrifying fashion, with batons, firearms, handcuffs, and prison cells. On the streets of Radom the police tracked down passers-by the way hunters track down hares with the battue. Human ribs and shins snapped like matchsticks. Hundreds of workers were held in cells in fearful conditions. The recalcitrant, ungrateful city was punished most insidiously: The building of new hospitals, schools, and apartment blocks was held up for years.

Those leaders of the workers' opposition in Radom whom the government considered most dangerous were killed in secret ways that to this day have not been brought to light. Many others were brought to trial, and the court proceedings were given the status of public events. The courts were to issue these people prison sentences, and an obliging press was to abuse them, vilify and humiliate them, calling them petty thieves, drunkards, troublemakers, rowdies. And that was how it was for a short time, for afterwards the situation changed radically.

There appeared some people who said, Enough already, to these despicable authorities. It was then, in connection with the Radom affair, that an overtly operating anticommunist opposition emerged in Poland. Its number included people of high standing in society, well-known and respected persons, and they acted as figureheads in this open opposition. And hundreds like me, ordinary folk, performed a range of tasks.

One of those tasks was to be present as independent observers at the Radom trials. The point was that even the corrupt, cowardly party judges were afraid of public opinion. So it could be hoped that in the presence of observers from outside of Radom, people who in ways known only to themselves were able to pass information to the western press, radio, and television, the judges would exercise more restraint and would not stoop to flagrant villainy. It didn't always work, but today, many years later, it can be said that those efforts were not without results.

So I was one of the observers who traveled to the Radom trials. A number of times I didn't make it, I was picked up on the way and held for twenty-four hours, and once I even got a drubbing with batons on the street in Radom.

Nevertheless, something was accomplished in those times.

And it was in Radom, under somewhat unusual circumstances, that I met Beata. She was a doctor in a hospital there, and she was deeply involved in the political affairs of the time. To people who'd been beaten up by the police she issued the necessary documentation without which it would have been out of the question to claim any compensation from the authorities. In fact, her affidavits weren't always a lot of use, and for her they only brought more aggravation. She had huge problems at work, she was in danger of losing her job, and she was forever being harassed by secret police officers giving her good advice: You should give all this court business a rest, ma'am, think about your future, you're young, you have a great career ahead of you, why are you fooling around, honey, and so on and so forth, but in such matters she was not a submissive person, she shrugged off their warnings, so once or twice so-called person or persons unknown vandalized her car, once or twice her apartment was broken into and the intruders smashed a number of valuable belongings and took a fur coat and jewelry, and when she demanded that the police investigate thoroughly, she heard in reply: Listen, pretty kitty, you don't bother us and we won't bother you.

Actually, that was a good name for her. She really was a
pretty kitty. Ruth, I'm sure you know those young, incredibly distinguished-looking cats, slim and lissome, with long
faces and big green eyes, the sort of seductive, neurotic cat
that emanates something exciting for half a mile around.
She was just like that, on the surface she was a good-looking woman, nothing more, yet she spread around her an
aura of constant tension, the air issued sparks in her presence, someone once said of her that the erotic energy she
gave off would have been enough to light up the whole of
Radom.

She was a tall, slim redhead with green eyes, she was all in
turquoise colors, that's how I remember her, turquoise and
amber, with an expression of sadness, or perhaps pensiveness, on her face. Her movements were slow, economical,
and precise, she spoke quietly but clearly; she rarely
smiled, but when she did it was a smile of indescribable
beauty, you could be excused for thinking that the whole
world was smiling with her, yet she had her secrets, maybe
even certain complexes from her past, which I was never
able to understand, much less to overcome, and perhaps it
was because of that that my love for her was unhappy. Perhaps that was why I failed, but I don't regret it because she
was uncommonly beautiful and deserving of love.

There was something unclear in her past, mysterious even,
for there were enclaves in her life, areas of feelings and
thoughts and even places to which she stubbornly and reso-
lutely denied access, with the proud anguish that usually

comes from the conviction that one is defending something unworthy of being defended, but that it must be done to maintain one's own dignity. For this reason I told her many times that her resistance was bitter, and her bizarre behavior encouraged the wildest conjectures and suspicions. Beata, I would say to her in the times when she was already very dear to me, You can't go on living like this, my darling. Your home is closed to me. I'm not permitted to go there. It's humiliating for me. She would reply calmly that she'd taken such a decision precisely so as to spare me humiliations. Obviously I wanted to understand what was going on. She assured me that she lived alone, so it wasn't a matter of a man or the traces of a man that I might come across in the apartment and feel painfully let down by. Then I would ask about skeletons in the closet. Everyone has some skeletons in the closet, so it's always good to know a little more, about which particular crime is involved. But she remained obstinately silent. Only occasionally, when I would insist too long and too forcefully, driven by anxiety about her feelings, by jealousy and suspicion, tears would appear in her beautiful green eyes, and I would say no more, frightened, for I could bear anything, but not her tears on my account.

I loved her then most tenderly, and I wanted to spare her any distress and worry connected with me.

We met rarely; after all, I lived in Warsaw and she in Radom, sometimes she would come up to the capital for a few hours, then at times I would travel to Radom, perpetu-

ally occupied by matters of great political significance, always rather tense and agitated, the aura around the two of
us at that time was almost always neurotic, we lived in a
stifling world of suspicions and threats, at every street corner the secret police could be waiting for us, I never made a
date with her like people do in the normal world because I
could never be sure whether I'd make it to the meeting
place. Two blocks earlier they might bundle me into a car,
or a few stops before Radom handcuff me and take me off
the train to be escorted back to Warsaw, where they would
release me amicably right at the station, with the look of
fun-loving buddies who've managed to pull another practi-
cal joke on a pal.

My meetings with Beata, then, were virtually conspiratorial
in character; the time of year didn't favor our plans, the
days were long, fine, and hot, the evenings sultry, pervaded
by bright sunlight, everywhere we went we were surrounded by crowds of people. This had its good side, because among large numbers of casual passers-by I wasn't in
danger of being arrested, much less of being beaten up, on
the other hand however there was no chance of our being
alone, of a tête-à-tête, of a kiss. I stole those kisses like a
schoolboy, on a park bench at dusk, in the gateway of an
apartment building we were passing, on an empty stairway,
and yet I wasn't a boy but a man in his forties, while she too
had her profession, her position, her magnificent, bewitch-
ing class. She was an elegant, cultured, highly intelligent
person, and we had found ourselves in a dismal situation,
something tragic and farcical at the same time, ambiguous

meanings, timidity, suppressed eroticism, and all this af-
fecting a woman who had an influence of unheard-of
strength upon me. Things became more and more unbearable, I kept telling her that it couldn't go on like this: Beata, I
would say, We're doing something terribly foolish, don't
take this too far, it's getting dangerous, that's what I said to
her, more and more agitated and in love with that beautiful,
unattainable woman, more and more deceived, and, something she seemed not to understand, abased in my own
eyes.

One day, towards the end of the summer, I found a haven
for us. It was the apartment of one of my friends from
Radom who had gone away unexpectedly, leaving a home,
a dog, and some potted plants for me to look after. It was
my job to water the flowers regularly and to take the dog
for a long walk three times a day.

The dark staircase, echoes rolling through it. We climb the
stairs slowly, Beata's ahead, I can see her beautiful calves in
fine dark panty hose, I can see her magnificent figure, the
woman's whole body is swaying in harmonious movement,
her golden red hair on her slender neck, her hand on the
banister, a bracelet on her wrist, a few more steps up, now
Beata is on the landing and has to turn slightly to the right, I
see her profile, delicate and fine, as if God had sculpted that
profile in a moment of exceptional inspiration, I see Beata's
lips clearly, there's a faint line of moisture on her upper lip,
I see her eye, which disappears suddenly behind a heavy
eyelid, Beata stops on the landing, turns to me and says,

Where are we going, actually? I don't actually fully understand. What don't you understand? I answer, but I can't go
on, she's standing right in front of me, filled with some terrible tension, waves of blood are coursing fiercely beneath
her skin. Where are we going? she whispers, Why do we
have to go there? Beata, I respond, I beg you, Beata, do we
have to go over everything from the beginning? What do
you mean from the beginning? she says and in fact she's
right, because there hasn't been any beginning yet, what's
happening between us now is supposed to become that beginning, we're at the beginning of the beginning, or maybe
even at the beginning of the beginning of the beginning, the
stairs have suddenly come to an end, they've disappeared,
the whole world is suspended in a void, I whisper once
again, I beg you, Beata, I look into her beautiful face, it's
more beautiful than ever before, then I say, Don't be afraid
of me, Beata, don't be afraid of me, to which she answers,
looking down at her feet, You know that I'm afraid of you,
I'm very much afraid of you. For goodness' sake, what are
you afraid of, my darling? You know what should be
feared, she says, it's an empty dialogue full of substance,
now I know that everything is over, there are no more stories in this building, I feel like crying in pain, the awareness
of losing a woman who is so desired, it's finished now, then
she says, You shouldn't jeopardize me like that, it was
wrong to do that. What, do what? I reply in a stifled whisper, and then something astounding happens, Beata turns
and continues up the stairs to the next floor, I hear the
barking of the dog, who has recognized me, neither of us
say anything, I open the door, the dark hallway, there's just

a strip of light from the living room, the dog nuzzles up to our legs, he's called Funio, Funio, I say, Funio, see how beautiful the lady is, a strange moment, I don't look at Beata, we go into the living room, it's a humdrum room, the most ordinary room in the world, we stand facing each other, her eyes are filled with tears, she says, Why did you do it? Do I deserve this? She turns to the window, now she's looking out of the window at the street below, I come up to her, we both stand by the window, the dog is nuzzling up and muttering, down below are frail little trees scorched by the heat, not much traffic, along the sidewalk comes an old woman carrying some bundles, a little farther off two men, gesturing animatedly, are talking together in front of a tobacconist's, incredibly slowly, filled with anxiety and shame, because I'm trying to be cool and sensible, I'm trying to take advantage of this extraordinary situation, and that's what I'm ashamed of, since I know that only spontaneity can save us, but I see spontaneity as a threat to my plans, it might be a word of hers, a gesture, a few steps towards the door, and then it'll be the end of everything, so filled with anxiety and shame I reject spontaneity, I mean to act coolly and according to plan, very gently I put my hand on Beata's shoulder, that's all, just that carefully calculated gesture, deliberate, so as not to scare off this woman, and then she says, Don't do that, you won't scare me off, so don't pretend, her words are like a slap in the face to me, a humiliation, a defeat, Beata says: I'm afraid because it's bad. Why bad? I say quietly. It's bad, she repeats, These things bind, we can't be bound to each other. I want us to be bound, I say, I want nothing more than just that. I'm afraid, she says, This is bad, it shouldn't happen, because we don't stand a chance, such things bind people too strongly, we mustn't do it, you ought to understand that it would be much better for both of us. No, I say, No, and I start kissing her greedily, roughly, painfully, I feel her resistance, she dodges out of my way, bows her head, but I'm stronger, she whispers, Please, not so hard, it hurts. Then don't move away, I exclaim, If you want it not to hurt don't move away, I know how to be tender and gentle, don't take from me what is best in me, don't condemn me to what is bad in me, I exclaim and hold her firmly in my arms, I feel her resistance weakening, but I've lost control over myself, all the weeks that have passed, all that terrible waiting has inclined me now to violence, I kiss her more and more painfully, I see her eyes, indescribably sad, for she's lost everything, all hope of some feeling that she could invest in me, she's already realized that it won't be me, that I'm no longer the person who brings hope, I'm already a stranger, more than during the previous weeks of fleeting rendezvous in cafés, on park benches, at those times she nourished the hope that at her side was a man, a bold and honest person, she had met me after all in the most unambiguous circumstances, she knew about my work, knew about my experiences in prison, she had touched my wrists from which the handcuffs had been removed only a quarter of an hour before, she knew who I was, she wanted me that way, but I was no longer that person, she didn't want me, I suddenly moved off and stood by the window, I looked down at the street, the men had vanished from in front of the store, a car passed, a boy came by on a bike, another car.

Silence, heat, the sun was slowly setting behind the roof-tops, its reflection in the windows of the building across the street, silence, I saw nothing, I was humbled, filled with shame and horror, because I'd realized that I was not on the side of the weak but on the side of the strong, that I was not on the side of the abused but on the side of those who abuse, I was humiliated, because I felt myself to be a cheat, but at the same time I could already feel in myself a touch of some miraculous hatred for this woman, for she was not without fault, she had no right to doubt and she shouldn't have uttered those accursed words, that we didn't have a chance, because for love there's always a chance, and when there isn't it's only because there isn't enough love, more love is needed and then there'll always be a chance, but Beata didn't know that, she was very beautiful and alluring, but she still hadn't suffered enough and that was probably why she believed there was something stronger and more important in a person's life than a man's love for a woman.

I didn't hear her leave the room. For a long time I stood at the window and stared at the darkening sky over that wretched, humiliated city. Like the city, I too was wretched and humiliated.

When it was dark, I put the dog on the leash and we went for a walk. Funio, I said, It wasn't our fault; besides, nothing's lost, Funio. That beautiful lady will still be with us. Funio listened attentively and indulgently.

But she never was with me again.

I continued to see her for some time, for a few months or so, till the beginning of winter. She always remained cool, polite, and implacable. I went on loving her for a long time. And then I began to think of her with aversion.

It was only many years later, in the midst of some splendid, sublime torment, that I found it in myself to forgive her. For it was I who had to forgive.

In the end, I was the one who had been wronged.

XVIII

I don't want to answer that question. It was dictated by your curiosity, and it seems to me to have a personal flavor, some maybe not fully conscious desire to know more about me, about my past. I mean, this has nothing to do with my experiences under communism that Gauting was so keen on. So what's this really about, Ruth? My answer will basically be an attempt at dialogue with your fear or, something that seems to me in fact to be very beautiful and precious, with your love. And so I want to ask whether this is the terrible moment of truth that always comes at some point to dispel illusions and prejudices between two people, or to put an end to certain longings?

I love you, Ruth, but we're not writing a screenplay based on my biography here. This is not at all about my inner life, full of demons, who formed me over a period of years and led me into temptation, but about a few simple truths concerning human cruelty, and about the fact that we are not equal to the challenges of the times.

What is it you expect from me? A confession that evil dwells within me? Of course it does, it's rooted deep inside me, perhaps deeper than in other people.

All right, Ruth. I'll tell you the story. But I know that certain matters are best left unspoken. There are unseen and unheard sides of the world in each person, and they should remain hidden. Even from that person's memory.

All right. I give in. I'll tell you.

I was still quite small then. I mean in terms of height, physical appearance. Nineteen forty-five, the end of the war, just after I left the concentration camp.

Don't interrupt me now, I beg you. You mustn't ask any questions now, express any opinions or doubts. This is what you wanted, so keep quiet and listen.

I'll tell everything as it was. I'll take you where I've never taken any woman in my life. In this sense you're becoming my Beatrice, though she was strengthened by the grace of God, and Dante himself was holding her hand.

I can't talk about this without an introduction, because here it's vital to draw in the background. I'm not trying to justify my actions. It's just that you have to know the world in which someone lives in order at least in some small measure to understand that person.

So I was short, physically weak, starving, maybe even at death's door, I was so debilitated. Before me I had a long journey back to Poland, hundreds of kilometers walking through woods, abandoned villages, burned-out towns. The war was still going on. The Third Reich was on its last legs. It was a time of fearful people and fearful reckonings.

We traveled in bands. At night the glow from the fires used to light up the sky. Everywhere there was the smell of burning. Never since then have I seen so many dead things. People and animals. Ruth, have you ever seen rotting horses? It's a brutal and evil sight, the whole of nature is concentrated in the carcass of a horse. A dead human usually seems smaller than when they were alive, in a human body there is a certain dignity, a little sadness, which inclines you to sympathy and reflection. But a dead horse is immense, it's no longer a horse but a huge alien mass, nothing but death.

We were always finding dead horses, great and terrible, though not sufficiently so for us to pass them by indifferently, because that was meat, and each of us hungered for a piece of meat. So we feasted; gathered around the campfire that illuminated the woods in the night, giving us a little warmth in those dark, cold depths, amid the pine trees creaking ominously, listening to the distant cannonade, we devoured tainted horsemeat. To this day I can remember that hellish taste. Rotten meat without salt, without bread, seasoned only with hunger.

We cursed our hunger, but after only a few days it seemed to us a blessed thing, because when it had passed our band was visited by fear, which is an even worse companion. Thanks to those horses I was sated after a fashion, and so I was afraid of every rustle, the sound of a twig snapping, a nearby shot. All about us in the woods there were half-wild German soldiers roaming around, who out of fear were prepared to kill anyone who appeared in their field of vision. They were pursued by half-wild Russians in long tattered greatcoats, with bloodshot eyes, gnarled hands, and the hearts of beasts that have gone hunting to settle accounts with the hunter who had been tracking and killing them mercilessly for all the previous years of the war. The Russians had no time to ask who was who. They fired without a word, uttering some lugubrious cry of despair, though it may have been just their triumphal laugh.

People for whom death had long been their daily bread were everywhere at large.

Prisoners from the camps, those who had been engaged in forced labor, people herded together from all corners of occupied Europe, and desperate deserters. These people wanted to eat, rape, burn, and pillage. The woods echoed with shouts, the crackle of burning trees, the howling of the wind, and the rattle of machine guns.

I slept lightly, always with my face turned to the fire. The nights were better than the days. By day I was accompanied by the stifling April heat, stinking of putrefaction and the soot of fires, of the spring that flayed the earth with morning showers then struck us in the back with the hammer of a scorching sun. The evenings fell all at once, as if they'd been tiptoeing up to the edge of the woods and then had come rushing onto the steaming purple fields. With nightfall there descended upon the earth a piercing, chattering cold of light frosts that turned to ice the remains of puddles on the tracks, lay white on the bark of trees, and hissed in the flames when we threw fresh pine branches onto the fire.

At that time I stayed around a Dutch boy who was the same age as me; he was well built, with shifty eyes, a thin nose, narrow lips, and hands that were in constant motion and were always bleeding because he was forever cutting them. He had sensitive skin as thin as parchment, yet he touched everything, as if he could only perceive the world through touch. There was a terrible desire in his hands, there wasn't a tree, a bush, or a stone on our path that he didn't wish to touch if only for a moment. The boy's face was almost completely white, as if it were covered in flour, but at times bloody red streaks appeared on it. Maybe he'd been beaten about the face while he was in the camp, maybe they were recent scars from whiplashes, because there was an SS officer in our camp called Reiner, stocky, dark-haired, always smiling and a little out of breath, I remember his crooked legs, tiny black eyes like two little coals, beads of sweat on his forehead, this Reiner had two dogs called Nero and Wolf, really vicious Dobermans, beautifully groomed, professionally trained attack dogs, Reiner always carried a hunting crop, he would strike the crop against his boot top, and then he would laugh cheerfully and somewhat hoarsely, and when he met a prisoner who was too slow in pulling the cap off his head, Reiner would strike him in the face with the crop, one-two, one-two, in an elegant, studied semicircular gesture that he had probably borrowed from the circus in better times, when as a boy he watched the lion tamers training wild animals in the ring.

At the time I'm talking of, Reiner was already dead, because our band had found him in some thick bushes at the edge of the wood one evening when we were on our way to the village to find some dead meat and bring it back to our campfire. Reiner fought desperately. Everyone fights desperately for their life. He had with him that famous hunting crop from the camp, he struck out with the crop over and over, terribly, I remember the crack of the crop in the air and the figure of Reiner, he seemed to me then oddly naked because he wasn't wearing his britches and uniform jacket but some dirty trousers and a shirt ripped at the chest, he was bathed in sweat as if someone had thrown a bucket of water over him, he struck out with the crop once, twice, ten, twenty times, pine needles were flying about, sticking to his sweaty face, towards the end he was virtually featureless, covered in needles like a wood demon, and then he fell, and we picked him up from the ground, someone grabbed the crop, someone made a noose out of it, I think it was actually the Dutch boy, and we hanged Reiner from a tree. Then we built a fire at the foot of the tree and we feasted, eating horsemeat and singing wild songs. In the end we lay down to sleep around the dying fire, and above us

Reiner swung in the wind, creaking over our heads, his shadow moving across the trunks of the trees around the fire, till it went out, till the hot gray ashes smothered the last little flames. At daybreak rain fell, violent, cold, and loud, a heavy April rain that broke the bough of the pine tree so that the hanged man slid down in a splash of water and a creak of wood right onto the extinguished fire. And when we woke it looked as if Reiner was one of us, a traveler sleeping by an extinguished campfire.

So we plodded on, sometimes down a forest vista, at other times along a dirt track across fields or through a village abandoned by its inhabitants, or even along the streets of some small town that bared fangs of blackened, burned walls. There were hardly ever any people there, because they were hiding in the woods or had fled while there was still time to bigger cities in fear of what might happen to them now. And to some it did happen. Thanks to that Dutch boy. One evening we decided to spend the night in a house that seemed to be the least damaged in the village. We even found some clothes hidden in the German wardrobes, and the Dutch boy, amazingly, turned up a few jars of jam from the previous fall. We lay down to sleep full and weary. It was a moonlit night, bright stars appeared in the cloudless sky, things went quiet all about, from time to time there was just the roar of the nearby artillery, or from somewhere beyond the woods the muffled chatter of machine guns.

I found it difficult to sleep in that silence, under that magnificent sky, the sight of which filled me with hope and restored calm to my thoughts. But it didn't last long. All of a sudden, around midnight maybe, I heard a penetrating cry. One cry, another. I jumped up. My traveling companions, still half-asleep but alert with the miraculous and terrible alertness of a perpetually frightened animal, opened their eyes too, some of them reaching for the knotted staves or rods without which no one went traveling in those days.

Someone struck a match and lit some dry branches, and soon a flame of light flared in the room, illuminating the blackened walls, the ceiling, and a door leading to a small upper story that had been burnt out.

Up there the Dutch boy had discovered two German women who hadn't had time to get away into the fields as we were drawing near the house.

To begin with they shouted a lot, but after the Dutch boy smacked them in the face a few times they fell completely silent.

Among us there was an old Frenchman, a strong man who'd spent four years in the concentration camp for being a communist, whether or not this was true or had been fabricated by the Germans. He had a large head bristling with short-cropped gray hair that hadn't grown back from his time in the camp, so that sharp little tufts of hair, like wild grass in the Mazovian fields, jutted out irregularly in all directions and looked a little like a devil's horns.

Bring them here, shouted the Frenchman. But the truth was he didn't know what he intended to do, because there was no bed in the room, no chair, even the kitchen stove was wrecked, and then there occurred a bizarre moment, an intense silence, like in the opera after the last chords of the prelude have died down, a silence of impatience and expectation before the first act, when it's dark all around, there's only a faint glow far off, and you can hear whispers, subdued breathing, and maybe even the beating of the music lover's heart.

At that time, in the intense dark silence, for the branch was barely glowing, I could smell in the room the familiar stench of the burning woods, see the outlines of human forms, and through the window, which had long been without a pane, a patch of dark blue sky filled with beautiful remote stars, I may even have seen the moon over the far-off tops of the pine trees, and I could hear in the distance the quiet, almost unreal rattle of a machine gun, from which someone was dying right then, shouting and invoking their mother or the Lord God, and right then the Frenchman made up his mind. He went up to the Dutch boy, took hold of one of the women, went to the window, bent the woman's body across the windowsill, spread her legs wide, placing her calves on his shoulders so that the woman's head rested on the grass beneath the window, and wheezing, smacking his lips, emitting grating sounds, moaning, growling, panting, like a beaten dog or a boar dying from a hunter's bullet, or like a man who for years has desired a woman who has spurned him and in return given him lashings, torments, and fears, dyings at dusk and at dawn, this was how he took that German woman, who remained silent and motionless, whose face none of us in the house could see because her head was outside, on that accursed German earth of wickedness and degradation, and I felt as if the woman's hair were drawing up from the earth the last juices of evil, as if through the woman's body there flowed echoes of what the Germans had done, as if through her body there seeped into the room the poisons of war, Jewish and Polish ashes, shards of French and Dutch bones, tufts of Russian hair, gold teeth pulled from the jaws of the bodies of those gassed and burned, and I also felt that I was on the other side, on the other shore, which was not my shore, where there was no more moon, there were no more stars, nor pine trees, nor winds, nor animals, nor people, but only the evil that has dwelt in humankind from the beginning of this world condemned and accursed by God.

And when the Frenchman had finished, the Dutch boy began. And when the Dutch boy finished, the Ukrainian began. And when the Ukrainian finished, the Pole began. Then another Pole. Then another Frenchman. Then the Gypsy. Then the Gypsy again. And then others, and still others, and still others. And in the end, when the first woman had stopped breathing and her body fell with a dull thud outside the house, some others took the second woman, who at first shouted and cried, pleaded and begged, and maybe also prayed to them, as if anyone in the world still believed in God and in the tables of stone, and it went on a long time, till everyone but me and a little old dying Jew, who was always crying, had given their seed.

The other woman survived; afterwards she lay beneath the window in silence, the moon upon her face like a bandage on a wound, her eyes wide open and blind, a wretched German, a wretched German woman of the last days of the war, a wretched human being.

And I was smacked about the face by my traveling companions, kicked black and blue and thrown out. You're not one of us, they shouted at me, in disgust and anger, you've betrayed us.

They spared the old Jew because he had been dying for several days, he was unable to take a woman, which made him pure and absolved. But I had shirked my duty and they couldn't forgive me.

There may have been some higher moral reasoning in that.

The next day at dawn I had to set off east alone, moving away from the black smoke of Berlin, from that night of shouting and abasement.

One day, now I'm getting to the crux of my story, I found myself on the outskirts of a larger town that had been almost completely abandoned by the Germans and was filled with hordes of Russian soldiers.

Among those ill-starred, courageous people many kind souls were to be found. One of them took good care of me. He spotted on the road a boy from a concentration camp; he recognized me at once by the clownish uniform and the skinny body. He came up and asked who I was. A Pole from Warsaw, I told him. Warsaw, he replied, I know it. I took it, or rather what's left of it.

He took me by the arm and led me to his billet. It was a small house with a little garden, well kept, trim, maybe three rooms, a kitchen, a pantry, and next to the house a barn and a pigsty.

The lady of the house was at home, a fairly good-looking, fairly young German woman whom the Russian soldier treated with a certain tenderness. Gerda, he said loudly, as if she could understand him, This is a Polish boy from a camp, your people tortured him, they beat him and starved him; now you're going to feed him, Gerda, now you are going to give him drink.

In fact she must have understood something, because she immediately began to bustle around me with a certain solemn hospitality. She laid the table in the kitchen, I remember the white tablecloth, the plate, spoon, and fork. The soldier went outside, all of a sudden I heard a burst from a P.M. machine gun, Gerda shuddered, there was fear in her eyes, she waited with her back to the wall to see what would happen next. In a moment the soldier appeared in the doorway holding two bloodied chickens in his hands. Gerda, he said, with these birds you'll cook some broth for the victors. Then she understood what was going on and set to work briskly, and the two of us men, like good farmers after a hard day's work, went out of the house and sat on the bench, the soldier rolled cigarettes out of shag tobacco and newspaper, and we began chatting.

He came from the heart of Russia, from somewhere on the Volga. He'd spent the whole war in the trenches, he'd been seriously wounded three times, they'd taken him to field hospitals, then he'd returned to the front line. A seasoned soldier, a simple Russian peasant who believed in God, in victory, and in Stalin. He had one ambition, to see Berlin burning, and that had passed him by since his unit had not got as far as the German capital, and others had taken it.

He sat hunched up on the bench, puffing away at the shag, which had the sharp, bitter taste of horse urine, he gnawed at his mustache and went on about the new order that would now reign on God's earth.

It was good to listen to him because he was saying good things, about people who would become good, about animals that would be bred by the good people, about good women who would bear the children of good men. And Gerda's good too, said the soldier, it's not her fault that she was born a German and that she was a dutiful woman to a German man. New times are coming now, he said, good times, and Gerda will become better, Gerda was going to bear him a child, although he'd never see that child, for soon he would set off on the long road back to Russia, where his wife might still be alive, though he couldn't be sure of that, the villages there had gone up in smoke, the people had perished, so he'd probably be alone on God's earth, though he would always have fond memories of

Gerda, who in a few months would bring his child into the world, a good child because it would be born after the war, of Russian blood conceived, from Russian loins brought to life.

The soldier went on like this while Gerda was busy in the kitchen. Finally she appeared before us and invited us to dinner. She was a little nervous; her hands were trembling when she poured soup into my bowl. I'd never had anything like it in my life. The soup had the taste of wormwood. The good soldier had shot through the chickens' gall bladders; the dish was indescribably bitter. But the soldier was good, I was good, the world was good, so we laughed the incident off, and Gerda treated us to army preserves, and, our stomachs full, we went on talking outside.

Evening came. It was quiet and mellow, like in peacetime, which had come again. The sun set lazily in a cloudless sky, then a gentle, warm wind blew up and ran across the shingles of the barn, and I listened to it intently and with a great unease, lying in the attic in the bed of a hard-working Prussian farmer, under a red eiderdown, with my head on a pillow for the first time since I could remember.

Night fell, quiet, warm, dark, empty. And all at once I knew that in a moment something would happen that would make my entire world different from that which had been given to me up till now.

Her footsteps creaked on the steep stairs that led to my little room. Then the door opened and I saw her figure on the threshold, but she seemed somehow huge to me, her head almost touching the ceiling.

They were both standing on the threshold. Gerda came up to my bed. She was wearing a long white nightshirt, she leaned over, took the hem of the nightshirt in her hands and began to lift it over her head; I stared at her thighs, her belly, at her breasts, I stared, petrified and sick, filled with desires and apprehensions, embarrassed and trembling, and then the soldier told me warmly and almost paternally to make room for Gerda at my side, he was giving me this woman taken from the enemy for this night, let it be my spoils of war, my well-deserved booty, because I had won this war, just as he had won it, for both of us had had our fill of troubles, of hard work, and suffering, and longing, I should take this woman, for she is a good woman, though she's from a bad nation, but she'll become better, life will make her better, life is stronger than Hitler and the bad people, so she has come to you to appease your hunger and to comfort you, so that at last you may fall asleep without suffering, without fears or specters, in a house that a soldier will watch over for your peace of mind and for your love.

And that was what happened. He watched over the house for me, and she gave me the love of a woman.

I don't know whether she spoke to me. Perhaps she was silent. When I woke at dawn, doves were cooing on the roof, but the woman had gone.

Early in the morning I set out once more, bidding the soldier farewell. Gerda didn't appear again.

Every woman in my life I remember in a particular way. Every one is present in my memory.

That first woman will forever remain a dove.

XIX

The little alleyway climbed almost vertically towards Schlüsselgasse, which was sparingly lit with neon lights. Down below, where the squat, dumpy building of the town hall stood, on Weinplatz, in the vicinity of the bridge that joined the two banks of the Limmat, it was brighter, the luxury stores glittered in many colors, in the window of a department store a beautiful girl was dressing a mannequin, her hair was the color of old gold, dextrous, slim arms and hands, long legs in dark panty hose. Kamil could see her thighs and her buttocks, squeezed into a short, very tight wine-red skirt. He stared at the girl; there was something erotic about her face, something brazen, she was well aware that she was beautiful, she was used to men undressing her with their eyes, she gave them a helping hand, she didn't leave them much work, but now Kamil's gaze seemed perhaps too intrusive to her, maybe she suddenly felt threatened, because she turned back into the store, said something that he couldn't make out, and right away by the entrance there appeared a tall, corpulent flunky in a navy blue jacket, gray trousers, balding, with a malevolent face and a dull expression. He measured Kamil with a challenging look, though with a certain politeness too, since he wasn't sure yet whether this person should be sent packing or rather invited inside with a smile to be shown a necktie or a shirt.

The square was deserted; there was only a stone stork, the symbol of a hotel, watching from the corner of a nearby building. Across the water on the Limmatquai cars were moving along, it was quiet, cold, the air bore the smell of the damp and elegance of Zurich, its sorrow and riches, somewhere far off a bell rang, here bells were always ringing, probably reminding people of their sins, and of the great difficulties that in this city are involved in the redemption of souls, the one thing that cannot be bought. It was quiet and deserted and Kamil decided that he could handle the corpulent flunky, guys like that aren't used to actual fights, what does he know about fighting when life or freedom is at stake, or best of all a woman, so he could handle him, even today, for he was still strong and fit, he had hard fists, swift arms, a jaw that had for years been accustomed to hard, painful blows, he could handle this poor little shop assistant, who looked like a worn-out ox, or maybe he was just a faggot, neckties, handkerchiefs in his breast pocket, socks with a dainty pattern, some good-looking young boy in a sports car with whom the old guy goes off somewhere south for the weekend, sometimes they even go far afield, all the way to sunny Tuscany, there are cosy little hotels there on the back roads around Siena, blinds on the win-

dows, a big deep bed, soft linen, the boy's skin is like a
Versace silk shirt, so he could handle this pansy who was
now standing challengingly in the entrance behind the
glass doors, and then he'd take the girl with him, maybe
to the Stork Hotel, or maybe he'd drag her into the back
of the store, where there are piles of soft, slightly dusty
but beautifully fragrant clothes, or quite simply, without
any further ado, he'd take her in the window, among
the mannequins, who would have more sympathetic expressions than those two, the girl and the flunky in the
doorway.

He lumbered off towards where Schlüsselgasse climbs
uphill, and in a moment he was back where he'd come
from, at the start of the narrow, steep alleyway.

"Where are you, man?" he asked himself. "And why
are you here?"

There was a man walking towards him. He was tot-
tering slightly, he'd clearly had a drop too much to drink
in the local bar. He was wearing a raincoat with the collar
turned up stiffly, and he had the gray, plastered-down
hair of a respectable bank clerk who spends the whole
day in a smart suit and tight shoes, then later, when he
gets home, changes into jeans, a colored shirt, and a
leather jacket with zippers on the pockets, and goes
downtown again, in his other incarnation, as a twenty-
year-old, a young buck, a boy, a member of the Youth International, which makes a mockery of the world. I could
take this one on too, thought Kamil complacently. One
kick in the backside and Mr. Deputy Manager is out of
the picture. Two kicks and it's as if he never existed. It's

my wonderful barbarianism that allows me to look upon the world so freely. Take the women by force, beat up the men, pat the children on the head, respect God, humbly obey the devil. It's my wonderful barbarianism, he said to himself, how much freshness there is in it! I could pull a great trick on them, that's for sure. All I'd have to do is to lie down here on the sidewalk, on this narrow little street, it's called Thermengasse. Lie down without a word, and die without a word. Tomorrow morning the sky would be rent with screams. Someone will come out of a nice house fragrant and preoccupied, and all of a sudden can't get past because there's a corpse on the sidewalk. Where are the municipal services, for goodness' sake, why wasn't this mess cleared away at once to spare decent people unpleasantness? But it'll already be too late, the ambulance will come, followed by the police. Gentlemen in trench coats, their hats perched on their heads, worried, unsure, even embarrassed, because right here, on this patch of good earth, where lives are lived honestly and in accordance with the rules of the best behavior, there is something as out of place as the body of a man without a name, without an address, without even a credit card.

Where I come from it used to be better, he thought. There at least there was always someone who'd try to rob the dead man, and if they bent down too soon then there was a chance of being saved. For even a thief would raise a hullabaloo if some guy were dying on a deserted street. And people would gather at once. Some of them would have an animated discussion about what bad times these are when you have to die on the street, as if your own bed isn't big enough for that. Others would try to help, and in this way quite a few folk have been dispatched to the great beyond, because instead of waiting patiently for a doctor, they would frantically begin artificial respiration through the ear, or pump streams of water through the sick man's barely parted lips. Yet they were guided by good hearts and love of their neighbor, which is always admirable.

Where I come from, it used to be worse, he thought, because they wouldn't even let you die quietly on the street of your choice, so as to gaze for one last time, alone, in peace and tranquillity, at the Warsaw sky.

The tipsy guy came up with an apologetic smile. He was perhaps fifty, his face weary, agreeably blank from the gin or whiskey, his eyes helpless, and Kamil felt ashamed that a moment ago he'd been thinking about this man with such animosity. He's one of us, he thought now, he is my brother.

"It's going to rain," said the man. "And it was so nice last week."

"Maybe it'll clear up," answered Kamil.

"No, it won't," the other repeated with drunken obstinacy.

They were now standing facing each other.

"I'm alone," said Kamil suddenly.

"Alone," the man sighed, drawing the word out. "So we can be together, eh?"

"Where's there a bar round here, pal?" asked Kamil.

"Just round the corner. But I'm cleaned out," replied the man.

"Never mind. I'll stand you a drink. And if you like I can even tell you my life story."

"I like to listen," answered the man. "I'm the kind of person who listens."

"Sometimes you bump into the right people," said Kamil.

He turned out not to be the right person at all, because after they had gone into a bar near the Münster, when they ordered drinks, took off their coats, and sat down at a table in the almost deserted barroom, with bored waiters wandering around and Rachmaninov on the radio, the stranger, instead of keeping quiet and listening, suddenly began saying bizarre things.

"My name is Aegli, Konrad Aegli, you can call me Koni. Imagine this incredible story. I have a good job, I mustn't complain. A house on the outskirts of the city, a pretty garden, friendly neighbors, though we're not real close. Which now turns out to be very smart. Because I have a wife, my friend, just like you I daresay."

"I don't have a wife," said Kamil.

"Is that so," said Koni Aegli. "I envy you a little. A single man. That always attracted me. How does he live, this lone man? Does he change women? There are different women in his life, he takes a trip to Geneva, there's a woman there, he takes a trip to Chur, there's a woman there, he goes home, there are women there too. And every one of them is different. I expect that's what your life is like."

"I don't take trips to Chur," said Kamil. "I'm not from here. I'm a foreigner, I'm from Poland."

"That doesn't matter," said Koni Aegli politely. "There are women in Poland too. Apparently they're very beautiful."

"It's been known," said Kamil. "Actually, I've been lucky."

"There you are, then," said Aegli, and smiled. "So that's how I'm going to live from today. My wife left me this morning."

"That's bad," said Kamil. "But what does it mean that she left you? She went out of the house in an unknown direction? Or did she tell you, as she cried her eyes out, that she'd had enough and was leaving forever? I'm asking because I have some experience with women who leave men in tears. If it was like that then tomorrow you'll find her at home. She'll cook you a roast with those little baked potatoes of yours. What do you call them again?"

"Roestli," answered Koni Aegli. "But she never goes into the kitchen. And she wasn't crying in the slightest, as for that, not in the slightest."

"That's not so good. How old are you?"

"Forty-three. Seventeen years of marriage. I never cheated on her."

"You must be mad," exclaimed Kamil.

"She's very beautiful, refined, she has quite a lot of money, she got it from her father, I always felt ill at ease with her father, but that's not what I want to talk about, so coming back to my wife, she never aroused my suspicions, we never fell out, we led a quiet life, and I'm a simple man, whereas she's real complicated, and that's probably why . . ."

"No, no," cried Kamil, who had suddenly begun to take this story to heart. "Don't look there for the reason. There's a man involved."

"I hadn't finished," said Koni Aegli with mild reproach. "Of course there's a man. A woman approaching forty doesn't run off to her daddy, even if her daddy is phenomenally rich and distinguished. She went off with a man much like me, but older, the most ordinary person in the world, the whole thing was a big secret all this time, it was only today I learned from her letter that a week ago she became his lover, he had given her a very great deal, you know, that was exactly what she wrote: 'He gives me a very great deal, you're not able to do that,' that's exactly how she put it, I could even have read it to you, but in that first moment of immense, indescribable rage I tore the letter to shreds, it's gone, not even that trace is left of my marriage."

All at once he gave a loud laugh. The waiter started; he made an ambiguous movement as if he wanted to come up, yet he stayed in his place, bending forward slightly, vigilant.

"And now I finally feel happy," exclaimed Koni Aegli.

"You feel happy," repeated Kamil, and suddenly felt a profound sense of brotherhood with this man, he knew now that Koni Aegli was entitled to that happiness, because he himself, Kamil, had experienced similar emotions many times in his life, when after weeks of ambiguous conversations, dark looks, stiff gestures, after nights of forced caresses and utterly empty days, he would all at once be alone, initially dulled and humiliated, then somewhat sad, and finally filled with a wild, intoxicating sense of regained freedom.

"I understand you, Koni," said Kamil softly. "Let me tell you something that may be crucial. According to you, she needs to have her man for life. That was how her daddy brought her up. She was let down, Mr. Aegli, maybe even not by you so much as by her own imagination. For women have imaginations when it comes to men. They have imaginations about us, we don't have imaginations about them. For us a woman is something concrete, don't you think? Legs, hands, hair, breasts, mouth. Occasionally a soul too, though not necessarily. But we don't create an image in our hearts that afterwards we seek doggedly for the rest of our lives. I understand you as few others do. We have no imagination, and for that reason one experience cannot be enough for us. Now, in your forties, you have a new second life ahead of you. In a few years' time you'll begin a third. It's a game of dice with God. Because He hoodwinks us terribly and mercilessly, Mr. Aegli. How can a person have only one life and yet at the same time be given so many different choices? Is that just? Can that ever actually be accomplished, Mr. Aegli? In this world there are thousands of beautiful places, women, jobs, things, but God gives each of us one place, one woman, and requires that we be content with what we have received, sometimes by pure chance. He enjoins us to practice moderation, and even to rejoice at what we possess, to rid ourselves of yearnings and above all of what God Himself equipped us with so we could live and make choices. For that's how things are. We're supposed to make choices, that's what we were created for, yet when we attempt to fulfil that obligation, when we begin to choose, in order to draw close to something, I don't know what to, but we have to draw closer, that's our primary obligation, maybe to redemption, maybe to peace, maybe to inner harmony, and so when we attempt to choose, God raises a hue and cry, calling our behavior sinful, irresponsible, base, and what you will, my dear Mr. Aegli. God made a botch of this world, but He won't own up, He saddles us with responsibility for all the shortcomings that arose during His work. I understand you. Now that she's gone off with your friend, you're free at last and can make choices without the fear that you'll become a sinner, for thank God, she's the one who has sinned, and you're at liberty to become a complete person."

"I'm beginning to think," said Aegli, "that you can't stand women."

"I love them," replied Kamil. "I love them too much. It's tough to live with that."

"Exactly," said Koni Aegli. "And that's why someone always has to leave."

He suddenly beckoned the waiter and ordered two whiskeys.

"We don't need to drink any more," said Kamil. "But of course I'll buy you another."

"I wouldn't dream of it," replied Aegli. "I wasn't telling the truth about the money. And as for my wife, I was exaggerating there a bit too. She's gone to stay with friends in St. Gallen. She'll be back the day after tomorrow."

"So what was all this for?" asked Kamil darkly.

The waiter brought two whiskeys and left.

"I like to open a conversation on a family topic," said Aegli. "But I have entirely different business with you. I'm a little hurt, I feel tired, I trailed around after you for hours through these Zurich side streets, I really was too shy to come up and talk, I've always been reticent in that regard, but it happened, and so I really want to ask you to hear me out, my dear sir. It's a simple, brief, and succinct matter. What it's about is that you should leave Mrs. Gless alone. You're right about the question of choice, no doubt about it. It may even be that your attitude to God is entirely justified; in that matter I'm not qualified to say, since I'm not a believer. It's true that it's not good to have to be content with what you possess, but it's also not at all good to reach for someone else's possessions. I want to stress that point clearly. Mr. Gless is a very understanding and honest man who cares about his reputation. He is involved in various concerns; any hint of impropriety could have adverse consequences for his long-term plans. Please don't be angry with me, I'm just earning my few cents. I've been hired, and I do what others require of me. So my request is short and polite. Finish off your whiskey, then we'll take a taxi to the train station, I have a ticket for you in my pocket, first-class, a sleeper, the bottom berth, to Warsaw, unfortunately via Vienna, but the transfer won't be too troublesome, there's only a fifteen-minute wait. Your luggage will stay here for the moment, we'll send it by mail from Geneva within a few days. Furthermore, in an envelope I have compensation for losses incurred as a result of curtailing your stay. I think we understand each other without words, so I'll wait now, please take your time finishing your drink, we have three-quarters of an hour before the train leaves."

"Are you done?" said Kamil calmly.

He held his whiskey tumbler at eye level and through the glass he stared at Mr. Aegli's face. It was blurred, pasty, a greenish color.

"Yes," replied Aegli.

"Is your name really Aegli?" asked Kamil.

"As a matter of fact it is, for your information."

Kamil nodded. He put down the glass, nodded again, and then looked the other man straight in the eye.

"Mr. Aegli," he said affably. "Nothing will come of this."

"Of what?" asked Aegli.

"You can eat your ticket to Warsaw," said Kamil. "And keep the envelope with the money to cover your expenses. If you refuse I'll give you a sock in the puss, my dear Mr. Aegli, like you've never had before."

"What are you saying," murmured Aegli, in some distress.

"We'll leave here right now and I'll rearrange your face in a fashion that this beautiful country has never seen. Then I'll rearrange Mr. Gless's face, not because he's worried about his wife, but because he's worried about her in a way that is insulting to her, which Mr. Gless probably doesn't understand because he's a stupid prick. Let me tell you something, Mr. Aegli. Up till this moment anything could have happened in this best of all possible worlds, as concerns Gless, Mrs. Gless, and me too. It could even have happened that I'd have gone back home to my country with a broken heart, leaving that beautiful, wise woman at the mercy of her future dreams, as fragile as her present ones. It could have happened that Mrs. Gless would have told me I wasn't right for her, in an intellectual sense, or because of the color of my hair, or because of my age, which seems entirely reasonable given the difference in our years. It might even have happened that I would have come to like Mr. Gless and would tell him that I'm a bad, dishonest man who has done a bad and dishonest thing, since I have not respected the sacred bonds of marriage and have slept with his wife, and for that very reason I'm suffering pangs of conscience. Yes, Mr. Aegli, up till now anything could have happened between us, but now only one thing will happen. Mr. Gless will get a kick in the backside, Mrs. Gless will get my love, and I'll get a rash every time I think of you, Mr. Aegli. And now you'll pay for all these drinks, since the person I invited to the bar was a stranger but a decent guy for whom I felt sorry for a moment, not some little stooge hired for a few hours by a wise guy grocery salesman, so now you'll pay for everything, because otherwise I really will smack you one, I may even knock you on the head with that coatstand, and then Gless will have to cover the costs of the damage to the bar. And don't try to threaten me with the police, Mr. Aegli. I obey the laws in this beautiful country, even here, despite the efforts of Calvin and Zwingli, nowhere is it written that you're not allowed to sleep with a woman if she has nothing against it. Otherwise Gless wouldn't have hired a little squirt like you, he would have sent some decent guys from the criminal police after me. And I'll tell you another thing, Mr. Aegli. I don't think she'll come back from St. Gallen after all. It's evening now, nearly eight o'clock, the right moment for what she's wanted for a long time, living with a guy like you. I'm almost certain that right now she's going to bed with a bearded, silent, uncommonly melancholy Russian émigré, and while she's about it she's uttering moans of ecstasy and cries of love such as you have never heard. And now I bid you farewell, in the name of all those humiliated and abased by so-called late capitalism, which is unaware of how eaten away it is by memory loss."

Kamil stood up from the table. He thought he might have to hit the other man, for Aegli wouldn't let him go just like that. But Aegli sat motionless, his face a little pale, his eyes narrowed. All of a sudden he said quietly:

"Well I never . . ."

And after a moment he repeated:

"Well I never."

And when Kamil moved off towards the door, the other man said calmly:

"Fine. I'll pay for the drinks. You see, sometimes it works, sometimes it doesn't. But we always have to do our job."

"And what would that be?" said Kamil from the door.

"That's easy," answered Aegli. "Now Mr. Gless can worry about it on his own. My part is over. I have just one last question for you."

"Try me."

"Is Mrs. Gless beautiful?"

"Very beautiful," replied Kamil. Then after a moment's thought he added quickly: "But I'm sure your wife is more beautiful. Don't pay any heed to what I said. Right now she's in St. Gallen drinking hot chocolate with her girlfriends. There aren't any Russian émigrés there. They all went back to Russia long ago. They left their false beards in the bars of Switzerland, they're hanging there now among the coats and umbrellas of decent Swiss, while they themselves went back to Moscow to wallow in democracy. Don't worry about your wife, she's a decent person. Actually," he added from the open doorway, "all women are decent. It's only us who are sometimes bastards, Mr. Aegli."

"Maybe you're right," said Aegli. "But it doesn't concern me. I don't have a wife. Not the first one with the rich daddy who left me today, nor the other one who sleeps with Russians in St. Gallen."

"You're nothing but a common lunatic," said Kamil, and walked out onto the street.

A warm wind was blowing. The neon lights were reflected in the low clouds sailing past.

Gless, thought Kamil, I didn't think you'd lose her so quickly. I had faith in you, Gless, in your Swiss calm and good judgment. I thought my business wasn't so important. But you ruined everything, for stupidity is the greatest enemy of love.

Now I'll never give her back to you. I'd die rather than give her back.

XX

"Schubert," implored Kamil. "I've never asked you for anything before, you've no cause to complain, but I have no more strength, so I'm begging you, please help me."

Schubert was silent. Kamil said:

"There's an excess of something in me. Too much secrecy. It's become unbearable. The explosion will destroy everything around. It's not about me. I can die. I won't lie to you, I'll say clearly and unambiguously that I don't want to die, but if that's a way out I'm prepared. I'm full of dynamite. One false move and that's it."

He spoke into the darkness; he could see Schubert's silhouette indistinctly against the swirling green of the shrubbery. It was only on the gentle slope of the Zürichberg that there were waves of street lights; a tramcar passed by quietly not far away, behind the cemetery wall a bird chirped after being unexpectedly woken.

"Listen to me, Schubert. I don't have any more strength to carry it inside me. Too much, too long. Oh, if only I could shout it out. You yourself know only too well what happens to someone who conceals terrible secrets. That perpetual, feverish hunt for a confessional, on every street corner you want finally to run into the person you'll reveal your mystery to. That's why I'm here. Who in this lousy world will listen to me if not you? I have no more strength to bear this."

"I can't help you with anything," said Schubert. "You know that."

"That's not true!" exclaimed Kamil. "You don't want to help me because you're turning into the bastard you used to be."

"I can't help you," said Schubert.

"If that's true, then it's better to go back to where the two of us were all those years ago. There at least a person knew that nothing, literally nothing depended on him. No one was master of his choices. Not me, not even you, Schubert. There was some deeper purpose in that, because why should someone have to have control over such terrible things, why should they take such terrible things upon their conscience, what does God have to say about that, with His much advertised charity and goodness. Listen, Schubert. Things can't go on like this. So either one way or the other."

"What does that mean?" said Schubert.

"She should die."

"Who?" asked Schubert coolly.

"Her. Let her die, because I can't stand it any more."

"Which her?" said Schubert.

"You know," said Kamil.

"You lousy coward," said Schubert. "You're the biggest bastard who ever lived. You won't even say her name out loud. You won't even take that much responsibility on those hunched scumbag shoulders of yours. It's all my doing, right? It was all Schubert, right? Well, let me tell you that those days are gone, once and for all. She's supposed to die? That's what you want? Be my guest. Slit her throat with a razor. Push her into the gas chamber, then toss the corpse out onto the fire. You know how it's done, man. These days the possibilities are endless, you bastard. You can walk into a store, buy a piece, and empty the entire magazine into her pretty little head."

"Don't talk to me like that!" shouted Kamil. "Don't you understand what's happening to me? You're not stupid. So let someone finally die, because in this crush I can never be certain of anything, in this crowd I'll never know peace. I repeat, if you want it to be me, I agree."

"Who needs you?" said Schubert. "Go back where you came from."

"But where did I come from?" Kamil exclaimed in desperation. "Can you tell me where?"

"I don't know," replied Schubert. "Maybe from hell."

Down below a tramcar passed by, lit up like a ray of hope. The bird called again from beyond the cemetery wall.

"Did you know that Joyce is buried here?" Schubert said suddenly in a mild, emotional voice, as if at some point in his life he'd actually met Joyce, or met anything that had a more human dimension.

"Joyce?" repeated Kamil. "Aha, Joyce. Right. But

when was that? In his day people were still able to live somehow. That's over now."

Suddenly he came close; now in the darkness he could see the outline of the other man's face, he stretched out his arm and grabbed Schubert by the lapel of his overcoat.

"Come off it," he said aggressively. "Come off it with your Joyce. I can talk with you about Dostoevsky even, but under different conditions. There have to be the right conditions for everything, you know that better than I do. So if you tell me now that you won't help me at all and that I should go back where I'm from, can you explain why you came to meet me? We're both standing here, and that must mean something. So don't give me any nonsense about Joyce, or Proust, or maybe Heine, none of whom you've read by the way, you haven't the faintest idea who they were, their names just caught your eye because you like to hang out in cemeteries. Say what you like, cemeteries are your favorite places."

"Nothing of the kind," said Schubert, and took a step backwards into the swirling bushes. It was even darker there. Suddenly Schubert gave a loud sigh.

"Your mind's all messed up," he said. "You've lost your sense of reality. What do you expect from me? I really don't have a chance now, all my chances have been used up, you shouldn't have done all those things that you kept doing against me. It's not that I hold it against you, I don't, it may even have been better that it happened like that, but I want you to understand that in the end things are as they are. You took part in it, you were even proud of it. Now it's too late."

"No," said Kamil. "It's never too late to do something that you used to do before. It's like a return, Schubert. People return home, return to their woman, they also return to themselves, so why shouldn't the two of us do so too?"

"Not any more," said Schubert.

"That's bitterness speaking," said Kamil. "And disillusionment."

"What if it is?" answered Schubert. "If it actually is bitterness and disillusionment? What's wrong with that? Are you the only one who's entitled to suffer?"

"Have you suffered, Schubert?"

"I have. Not any more, though. And that's why I say it's too late."

Suddenly he shivered as if he'd been taken by a chill, and said:

"I'm not going to stand here forever. If you want to talk to me some more, we'll have to go down. I've no intention of spending half the night traipsing along dark alleyways just to suit you."

"All right," agreed Kamil. "Let's go down. This is a big city, you can get lost in it."

"I have no desire to get lost," retorted Schubert.

Kamil went downhill in a gentle arc; to begin with it was completely dark and deserted, then there came the growing hum of the city, which surrounded him on all sides, cars appeared on the roads, pedestrians on the sidewalks, then he crossed Ramistrasse, where there shone green, blue, red, and yellow neon signs, near the theater he passed a number of good-looking women who smelled of cosmetics, at that point Schubert said:

"I like it here."

Kamil continued to move ahead, it got dark again, it was only on Bellevue that he suddenly found himself in a network of bright lights, he looked good, a tall, slim man, he kept himself in great shape, a fit figure, youthful movements, beautiful fair hair over his forehead, a straight nose, narrow mouth, healthy teeth, a really good-looking man, he had something of the look of a beautiful animal, a horse maybe, a leopard, he held himself straight, walked with an even step, he looked great, people were inclined to trust him, to like him, and also to admire him somewhat.

So he walked along at an even pace, fairly quickly, at one point Schubert said:

"You don't have to pretend."

"I'm not pretending," replied Kamil.

But he slowed down a little. He crossed a bridge and went down Bahnhofstrasse, in the elegant sparkle of the lights, in the multicolored human throng, in discreet and pleasant fragrances, and then Kamil said:

"I had a dream about you, Schubert."

"What dream?"

"A bad dream."

"Only a bad person has bad dreams," said Schubert tartly. "And?"

Kamil stopped in front of the window of a chic stationer's. It had turned a little colder, and when Kamil spoke his breath settled in a delicate film on the pane. Schubert stood right next to him, somehow reluctant.

"You were a messenger," said Kamil. "You were wearing a yellow frock coat, a dark blue top hat, and high boots that were tight around your calves. The messenger came at dawn. His horse was steaming, lobes of foam were falling from his rump onto the freshly mown grass in the orchard."

"What orchard?" asked Schubert.

"It was my orchard. The messenger handed me some documents. It was a renunciation. I was to sign a renunciation."

"What renunciation?" asked Schubert. Kamil's breath settled like a tiny little cloud on the surface of the glass.

"I was supposed to renounce her. I was supposed to sign and say that I renounce her. I refused. The sun was rising. The whole sky was red. Then you said that my renunciation no longer had any meaning anyway, because her head was to roll at dawn. You pointed at the sun and said that now I could sign anything, because a moment ago her head had rolled into the basket on the scaffold."

"And did you sign the renunciation then?"

"No," said Kamil. "I cried. But I felt an enormous sense of relief. For it hadn't been me who was responsible for her death."

"I don't know," said Schubert. "Maybe you."

The film from his breath flashed purple on the window pane.

"Did I ride off somewhere else?" asked Schubert.

"No. All of a sudden you did what you did once before."

"What did I do once before?"

"You tore my heart out. It didn't hurt, but you tore it out."

"In a dream," sneered Schubert. "For the second time in a dream. Now there's a thing . . ."

"This is a dream too," said Kamil. "But a different one."

"I wouldn't mind a bite to eat," said Schubert. "Dream or no, I wouldn't mind a bite to eat."

Kamil continued towards the train station. A tramcar passed, it pulled up at a stop, people got on and off. Schubert said:

"So you don't have any more strength. You can't handle it, eh?"

"I can't handle it. Actually nothing special is happening. The days pass quietly. Ruth loves me."

"So what's it all about?"

"I don't know. There's an evil in me, Schubert. A terrible evil dwells in me."

"It dwells in everyone. It has to be driven out. Maybe you should go to the Lord God with this business? He helps sometimes. You can't tell when, where, or why, but at times He helps, at others He doesn't, it does happen. So it may be worth giving it a shot. You did it once before, it even worked a bit."

Schubert suddenly broke off and gave a harsh, unpleasant laugh. But in the crowd on the street no one paid any attention to his laugh or his rather boisterous behavior.

"What is it?" asked Kamil uneasily. "What is it now?"

"Don't pretend," said Schubert. "You can pretend with anyone, but not with me. I wouldn't mind a bite to eat. Is this a bar?"

"It's a jeweler's. There's a bar next door."

He went in, took a seat at a table near the door, and asked the waitress for a prawn cocktail and a Cellier des Dauphins.

"I remember your prayer," said Schubert quietly. "I don't think I've ever seen anyone pray so fervently. And what came of it? Did you save your soul?"

"Give it a rest," said Kamil. "That was years ago."

"A long time ago," answered Schubert. "But I remember every detail."

He leaned to his right and reached over to the next table, where crimson and pale green boxes were set out. He opened the nearest one, the lid rose dutifully, inside on a soft, wrinkled velvet cushion lay a diamond necklace with a fine-wrought clasp. Schubert picked the necklace up, weighed it in his hand, then put it calmly back in its box. He took a sip of wine, narrowed his eyes, and his face lit up. He really looked quite young and attractive.

"It was a hot day," he said pensively. "In springtime such hot days are usually pretty rare. It was almost sweltering, remember? They came out of the middle of the woods, completely unexpectedly, I couldn't do a thing, I was taken totally unawares, so I stopped on the trail as if I were paralyzed, I remember you gave a ferocious shout, an indescribable shout . . ."

"That wasn't me," said Kamil. "It was the others who were shouting."

"You too, I remember well. How many of you were there?"

"About seven, maybe eight."

"The shouts of eight little bastards. You were the

smallest of them, you were a little shortass, you were knee-high to a grasshopper and already you were shouting in the most murderous voice I've ever heard."

He took another sip of wine; an expression of concentration and sorrow could be seen on his face.

"The sun was lighting up the tops of the trees, pines they were, tall, brown, slim, like in my childhood. The other guys stood somehow indecisively, but after a moment they realized what you wanted. It was you, shortass, who was shouting loudest for the Russkies to shoot me dead. Kill him, you were calling, shortass, kill him. Was that not how it was?"

"That's how it was," said Kamil sourly. "And what of it? Tell the truth, Schubert. Come on, tell the truth for once. You were going to waste us all in those woods. You hadn't the slightest intention of escorting us to Lübeck or whatever, or to anyplace else. Tell the truth, Schubert, and don't play the innocent. You were going to waste us with that Schmeiser of yours, you'd even lost your spade on the way somewhere so you couldn't have buried us, at most you'd just have tossed a bit of turf over the stiffs and then off into the woods, just trying to lose those Russkies. So perhaps you could see your way to exercising a bit of moderation and restraint in this little tale. What do you want from me? Yes, at the time I wanted the Russian to pop you. I prayed for it. I prayed fervently."

"But God didn't heed your prayer, huh, shortass. . . . God wanted to be crueler than those Russkies in the woods. Do you remember what you did to me?"

"I prayed for your death, Schubert. And I don't regret

it for a moment. Who was it who beat me over the head with a shovel till I lost consciousness? Who ordered that punishment of twenty lashes with the whip to be repeated because I made a mistake in the counting, I was supposed to shout out the numbers loudly and clearly, and by the sixteenth I was barely conscious, and I made a mistake, and you ordered Reiner to start again from the beginning. Because of you then I got more than thirty lashes, you bastard. So don't play the saint with me, Schubert. I know you."

"Who's playing the saint?" exclaimed Schubert, and ordered two more Cellier des Dauphins and some sapphires on a little plate. "The difference between us is that I never denied my actions. Actually, even if I'd tried to, people like you would never have let me get away with it. But today maybe you'll admit what you did to me in those woods. Besides, I don't hold it against you at all. After all, I survived. Unlike Reiner. That Reiner was a son of a bitch, there's no denying it, but to finish off a guy like that, come off it. . . . That lost SS unit that was desperately tramping around the woods between the canals of the Spree, they heard my last cry. The cry of a dying man, a man being murdered, shortass, which you wouldn't listen to, you were so busy praying. I remember your faces. You were enraptured as you were digging my grave, and the Russkie was urging you on with shouts. You dug that grave with your bare mitts and your bare fingers, because there was nothing else on hand, you pulled the soil out with your teeth, shortass . . ."

"Don't call me shortass, I'm not a shortass."

"But you were then. You were knee-high to a grass-hopper. How old were you then, on the day you tried to kill a defenseless man with your bare hands? How old were you then? Fifteen? Sixteen? You started early, shortass."

"Don't talk to me like that," exclaimed Kamil. "It was an act of justice."

"An act of justice," Schubert repeated mildly, almost touchingly. "Is that what you call it in your language? When seven kids tie a man to a tree, and then intend step by step, methodically, slowly, to tear off his arms and legs, then his penis, then gouge out his eyes with a stick, bite off his tongue, ears, nose, and lips, with their own teeth, then bury what's left in the ground, so that only the head sticks up above ground level, in your language is that called an act of justice?"

"Schubert," said Kamil in a tone of persuasion. "Listen to me carefully. You were one of the worst murderers to have walked this holy earth. You killed hundreds of people in hundreds of different ways, and it was never enough for you. Maybe you're partly right, that at that time we were carried away by a low desire for revenge, for decent, level-headed people would have handled things differently, we could have too, all we had to do was to ask the Russkie to shoot you or to hang you from the nearest tree. And everything would have been as the Lord God commanded. We would still have sung for joy and thanked heaven for what it had given us, but in no way could you question that incident as an act of historical justice. You didn't deserve any better."

"Who did? Maybe you? Don't you understand that

anyone who survived it all lost the right to survive it all? Do you still not understand that, shortass? All these guys here I find ridiculous and hypocritical. They sit in this café, in a thousand other bars all over the world, and complain bitterly about people like me because I was mixed up in Jewish matters during the war. But in a short time nobody will be mixed up in those matters at all any more. Nothing lasts forever. If we wait another fifty years it'll turn out that the Jews massacred each other, or that they disappeared and went to the moon. If we wait a while it's bound to happen, because people don't like to think badly about themselves, they've always considered themselves to be high-minded, righteous, and filled with the fear of God. The crematoria and the gas chambers will be covered by sand brought in on the desert winds of oblivion, and nothing will be left of all the bones. And only then will everyone breathe a sigh of relief. Even the Jews, for they long for that too. Take up jogging, shortass, and you'll live to see those good times. By then they'll be killing off someone else, maybe the whites, maybe the blacks, maybe the yellow people, and maybe at last the time will come for the angels and for the Lord God Himself to have His throat slit. But today no one should pretend that they weren't involved, shortass . . ."

"I wasn't involved," said Kamil.

"Yeah? You weren't involved? Then perhaps you'd be so kind as to drop your trousers."

"What are you talking about, Schubert? You must be mad."

"I'm talking about the fact that if you weren't involved, then today you should have a clipped willy."

"What are you going on about, Schubert?"

"I know you all," said Schubert sourly. "Everyone mentions the Holocaust a hundred times a day, in a hundred human languages. But I ask you, if an old, pious Jew dies in some town, in the whole area, for a radius of a hundred miles from his death bed, where will ten other pious Jews be found to recite the Kaddish for the dead man? Where are those ten Jews who are essential to the eleventh Jew who has just died? Just imagine, they don't exist. They're never there. Even in places where they once constituted a huge majority, today it's like looking for a needle in a haystack. All around there are nothing but pious and sympathetic Christians. Let me tell you something, quite frankly. At least I don't pretend. The Jews always got on my nerves, I couldn't stand them, me more than most. And then it happened. Maybe it wasn't entirely fair, because there are different kinds of Jews, some are even really nice people, there have even been some good-looking Jewesses, and there were quite a few of them who were real smart up top, in a word some things are missed, there were losses, and that's to be regretted, at any rate I regret it sincerely now and I feel partly to blame, though it wasn't me who thought up the Holocaust. But others? The high-minded? Where were the high-minded then? They were sitting in some dark corner trembling for their own lives. You trembled too in fear for your own life, don't say it wasn't so. These days everyone's become dreadfully civilized and they curse those who made the Holocaust. But such curses cost little. While to make good the loss, to repair history a bit, that's too much for them. Penance? Let me tell you simply,

I come from a simple family, my father was a miller near Titisee, a lovely area by the way. If the Christians regret what happened so much, there's only one thing they can do. Become Jews. It's not so hard. Tables of stone and an ordinary knife. And you're a Jew. And then the pious old Jew can die anywhere, without worrying that it won't be possible to find a handful of other pious Jews to recite the Kaddish for him. But no one's prepared to do that, because it's not at all convenient to be a Jew, not even today, after all that happened, even in this café, in the very center of this nice city. If you're of a different opinion you can prove me wrong. You can shout aloud right now that you're a Jew and that the Christians are responsible for murdering millions of your Jewish brothers. Please, do it. Do it right away. In five minutes you'll have that goddam democratic Zurich police down on you. And maybe a few guys from the local loony bin. Do it, shortass."

"I'll do it," said Kamil. "But if I do it, you'll help me."

"You're a worse bastard than I am," said Schubert. "But if you do it, I'll help you."

"You were shouting," said Ruth. "You were shouting terribly."

He lay now with his eyes closed. He thought that it wasn't over with Schubert. I'll get you, Schubert, he thought. And you won't wriggle out of it this time.

"Don't think about it," said Ruth.

Now he opened his eyes. Maybe I don't have the strength to save myself, he thought. But I have the strength to love her.

"Love me," she said almost commandingly.

He smiled shyly, like a little boy.

"There's nothing that I want so much. Because if there's anything that is still my life, it's only that strange love for you," he said quietly, and put his arm around Ruth. He smelled the fragrance of her hair. He was back here, in this slightly better world of his bitter waking hours, which were ripped and coming apart at the seams like a downtrodden rag, full of filth, shame, and weakness, and yet somehow ordered, where a table was only a table, a wall a wall, where even he was partly himself and no one else.

"Once, years ago, I found myself in Zurich," he said, stroking the woman's hair. "I remembered parts of the city. There are streets there peopled with specters. I was dreaming of Zurich just now. And of your husband."

"Gless isn't often in Zurich, but he's from there. He settled in Geneva years ago, he has no more connections with Zurich."

"I connected him," said Kamil, and laughed with a painful pride.

For a long while they lay in silence. Suddenly Kamil said:

"Is Aegli a Swiss name, what do you think?"

"Yes," she said. "You met him at our house. He's one of Gless's directors."

She fell silent, then a moment later added:

"I like him. He's well bred. A little shy. But he handles difficult, unpleasant matters that my husband prefers not to get involved in. Every company has someone like that."

"Yes, I remember now. A tall, broad-shouldered guy, looks a bit like a boxer."

"That's him," said Ruth.

"Koni Aegli. The guy for dirty business."

"I wouldn't go so far as that," she said. "Gless doesn't do that sort of thing. Aegli handles matters that require assertiveness and obstinacy. But why Koni? His name's Simon. Good-looking, stylish, resolute, and at the same time shy Simon Aegli."

"My God," said Kamil. "I've flipped."

It didn't sound like a joke. There was a gloomy, apprehensive tone in his voice. Ruth looked into Kamil's face concernedly.

"I'm like a burned-out house," he said quietly, and closed his eyes. "I don't think I can live any longer. Even the ruins that are left within me are smoldering constantly. Too much, Ruth. Too much emptiness, if you can understand that."

"Don't think about it," she said. "Think about me. It's really so simple."

"You're right," he replied. "It's so simple."

XXI

The shadows drifted across gently, exceptionally quietly, as if they were not there. And the light was noiseless, filtered through the net curtain that moved slightly in the wind and parted, revealing shamefacedly, perhaps even with a little humility, the boulevard glistening with moisture, a fragment of the roadway along which cars were driving affably, and a bit farther, as it were in the wings of the city, the outline of the bridge that led towards the machine by the lake. Higher up the neon lights were on, massive but delicate, partly shrouded in mist and also very quiet. Everywhere silence reigned, you couldn't hear the wild animals roaring in the bush, young children crying, abandoned and left prey to evil, you couldn't hear anything, silence reigned unbroken, right now she was crossing the street below, beneath the windows, a slim, dark woman in a long dress, with stunningly beautiful hair and even more beautiful eyes that made you think of the boats of fishermen in the Gospels. She came along the boulevard, stifling every sound around her, the cars were traveling as if in a dream, the waters of the

Rhône soundlessly washing the concrete embankment, even close to the bridge, where the desperate foam was forever swirling, even there the silence was present.

And only Kamil knew why it was so.

Look, Schubert, he thought, I've found myself at the end of the world, where I was never supposed to be any more. She did it, thanks to her I'm here again, secure, sad, filled with guilt and silence. What has she saved me from, Schubert, what do you think, he asked in silence. But he knew she had saved him from his memory.

"Ruth," he said very quietly, or maybe he didn't actually say it at all, since she could hear his thoughts anyway. "I'd like to have a gesture of love. Can you give me that?"

"I can," answered Ruth.

In the room now it was quieter still, even God had tiptoed out, closing the door behind Him. Ruth leaned over and took hold of Kamil's head. She held it in her strong, yet very frail and delicate hands and looked searchingly into his face. Her eyes were for him like sailboats on Galilee, or like the life rafts on the Titanic, the last hope of the shipwrecked. Kamil thought that God shouldn't have left, if He'd stayed in the room He might finally have learned something about the goodness and courage of the woman He had created from the rib of a man.

The wind blew the curtain to one side. A car driving down the boulevard bid them politely good evening. The bright patch of the headlamp summoned Ruth's profile from the darkness. Suddenly Kamil felt her touch grow stronger, now her hands were holding his head so firmly that it almost hurt.

"Say something," he said quietly, though he didn't

want that at all; for her gaze seemed more important to him than any words. He saw in her eyes that which he had been waiting for for so long, a life for him without fears and torments, all bad deeds forgotten, sins forgiven, and virtues rewarded.

So he thought that that was what redemption looked like, and that terrified him, because he didn't want redemption, he only wanted this woman. Nothing else.

He gave a profound sigh. It was almost a moan, for she said:

"It can't be."

"What can't be?"

"It can't be such a torment for you," she said.

She was still holding his head in her hands; she was leaning forward slightly, fiercely beautiful with her triangular face in the motionless half-shadow, in the silence of the boulevard along which the affable cars were driving, in the wail of sirens announcing the sinking of transatlantic liners and galleons, in the thunder of the thousands of feet of those who had passed through the gate at Birkenau, trodden the paths along the banks of the Irtysh and the Lena, by the edge of the taiga and the snow-covered fields, in the dull rumble of transport trains on the tracks, when amid mist and cries the lights of the signals were turned on, Karaganda and Treblinka, Komi and Sachsenhausen, and maybe even earlier, when the tumbrels from the Conciergerie rolled slowly down the street, and in just such a final, enclosed silence, the heads fell into the executioners' baskets, she was then fiercely beautiful and longed for, and Kamil said with intense emotion:

"There are two things I want to tell you."

"Tell me," said Ruth. She still held his head in her hands, as if she were saying farewell to a dying man.

"I want to tell you how beautiful you are, and I want to tell you what my love is about."

She went on holding his head in her hands; it was the most wonderful caress he had ever known, because it was not a caress but an act of possession, holding Kamil's head in her hands this woman took this man for herself, what better thing could he dream of than of becoming a hanger for her dresses, her toothbrush, or the air she breathed.

"You are beautiful," he said, "but in a different way than all the beautiful women I have ever seen. They were very physical, and it was in that that I found the beauty. With you it's different."

"Do I not have breasts, arms, hands?" she said, and laughed mildly. "I have hands, Kamil."

She made a tender gesture, passed her right hand across his cheek, but he had precisely a feeling of incorporeality, as if a thought had touched his face. He looked into Ruth's eyes.

Lord, he said to himself, why are You giving me this? I'm an old blasphemer, I've been abusing You for decades. I might even have made fun of You when You were especially weak. So why are You giving me this?

He suddenly began talking to God the way you talk to your next-door neighbor, simply, without fear, in ordinary, everyday language, with gratitude, with incredulity, How could this be, he said to God, did I help You up when You fell in the dust and heat on that steep road, did I wipe the sweat from Your brow when You were suffering, as You walked then to the hill of torment and death, I was one of those who mocked You, I may even have thrown a rock at You, I was shouting at You at the very moment when she was near and wiped Your tortured face, wet with sweat and blood, so why are You giving me this today, in the name of what are You giving me it, and for what reason, since I really haven't deserved anything but anathema and loneliness.

"Nothing's going on that might be a torment," said Ruth. "Look at it all. The chair. You can see the chair, Kamil. And you can see the table too. There's a picture on the wall. A reproduction of a Klee if I'm not mistaken. Yes, Klee. The parted curtain, Kamil. Does that cause you pain? Behind the curtain there's just the normal, stupid world. It's really nothing out of the ordinary, I mean it's not like you've come to hell. The Rhône isn't particularly beautiful here, it always roars as if it were furious, but it's not dangerous. So do you really have to be so distressed?"

"No, I don't," said Kamil. "But I think something's broken in me, some little cog is out of order, so many years in top gear, remember that, for so many years my soul has been ravaged beyond measure, so is it surprising that it can't cope any longer, maybe something has cracked, Ruth, maybe I only have half a soul left, and the other half was taken by the devil, whom you know nothing about here. And don't talk to me about torment. In life nothing comes for free, people here are well aware of that. So I look at you in this room. So I look at you. So I look. And I see your beauty, I see your eyes, Ruth, and there's so much of your hair that all the angels of our northern hemisphere could drown in it. So I see you, Ruth. And I pay for that. You say it's torment. Then let it be. I give you the name Torment. I baptize you Torment, in the name of the Father, the Son, and the Holy Spirit, amen.''

Once again he looked silently into her eyes. And he saw in them, as never before in his life, a feeling of great love. That was why he said after a moment:

"Say it."

She shook her head.

"Say it," he repeated, and she shook her head once more.

"All right," he said. "You don't have to say anything."

He took her head in his hands, buried his fingers in her hair as if he were diving into the ocean. He kissed her.

God, he thought at the moment of that kiss, how can it be that I am all in her and she is all in me? How is it possible, as soon as I touch her lips with mine, move my tongue, find her tongue and they are joined, slowly, gently, delicately, in silence and darkness, and yet I see her now whole, I am all within her, deep down, in the dark places where she carries the warmth of life, where there is the beginning of everything, in the pulsating, damp, hot cave of God, from which He drives people out into the world, into emptiness and conjecture, fears and soothings, I am in the place where God has His dwelling, you just have to cross a gentle little hill to find an open gate, and there is a shining, pink passageway full of heat and joy, smooth and straight, and farther on is a great hall of cries, and farther a great hall of moans, and a great hall of murmurs, touches, looks, and fragrances, and finally there is a tall, narrow, steep staircase that you have to climb slowly all the way to the top, where, impatient and joyful, a man's last breath awaits.

She tipped her head back. She had a joyful smile on her face. She spoke very quietly, in a whisper, maybe worried that she would wake him up, or maybe hoping that he wouldn't hear her words.

"I love you, Kamil," she said.

She half-closed her eyes. The thought came to Kamil that he wasn't good to her, that he demanded too much of her, he wanted those words from her, and she was one of those women who are afraid of words. Perhaps they're right to be, words have great causal power, they're more significant than thoughts and deeds, maybe she was right to fear words, there was something in her past, probably that old man or Gless a few years ago, or someone else, some cries, whispers, names, so she was entitled to avoid certain words, and yet she had said something of immense importance, she couldn't take it back, and that was why Kamil felt guilty.

Once again he buried his fingers in her hair, as if in dark waters.

"Listen, Ruth," he began. "You said it. But you're still in no danger. I want you to understand what my love is about. I want nothing for myself. I know one thing, Ruth. I'll never let you suffer. Ever. Anywhere. Because of anyone. I don't want that. I have chosen. If bad is to happen, it will only happen to me. For me will be the worse share. That's still a great joy for me, because in that worse share there will be a part of you. That's enough. So don't be afraid. No wrong will befall you, no pain will reach you. Nothing in this world is worth as much as ordinariness, Ruth. I've never known it, perhaps that's precisely why I love you so much, because with you I find a piece of the ordinary world, I hear the voices of children, their laughter, and also maybe Gless's over-dignified steps, at bottom he's an entirely decent man, lost, in fear and pain, condemned to suffer, but someone always suffers when there's love between people, that's how things were set up in the world, I really feel sorry for him now, I didn't mean to make him unhappy, but I know that's how things have to be among people, it hurts me to think about him. Not long ago he was the object of my envy, maybe even outright hatred, and yet he's a decent man, your Gless. I was never like that, even when I wanted to be, and I tried with all my might, but I didn't stand a chance, there was always some devil, or some whore, or some villain who put a spoke in my wheels, and once again I became the startled victim or the stupefied executioner. I don't have the kind of life that could go with yours, Ruth. There's nothing I can give you but bad luck and misery. Really, I have no right whatsoever to talk to you of love, for what is it worth, what can the feelings of a cannibal who's come to you from the ends of the globe be worth? Yet if it is worth something, then I think it's that little bit of madness thanks to which we sometimes become like gods."

He fell silent, and closed his eyes. Down below the cars passed noiselessly. Next to him he could hear Ruth's quiet, joyful breathing.

Schubert, he said in his heart, you can see me now, and you know full well that if I keep her, I'll be redeemed.

XXII

The bridge was bright and beautiful, strung low across the lake. A person leaning on the metal balustrade had the impression that it was enough just to stretch out an arm in order to touch the mirror of the water with their fingertips; the cars moved laboriously along the wet roadway of the boulevard, the neon signs of banks greeted the passers-by, from the mountains there blew a gentle wind that smelled of the meadows, far off the fountain spouted, huge cascades of white, glistening water fell from way up onto the surface of the lake, a ship flying a French flag was leaving the port and setting a course for Evian. The evening was warm, elegant, and solitary, in the streets of the old town, in the sparingly lit alleyways, where at every step there were nice cafés with good wines, efficient waiters, and silent customers, in those picturesque little streets that climbed steeply upwards, here and there creaked tiny little scaffolds, and the discreet swish of the falling blades of guillotines could be heard.

He felt a great, almost blinding joy at the thought that

he could drown here, one step was enough, there were metal stairs leading down to a metal footbridge, walkers crossed it with their dogs to get to the island, but you didn't go to the island, you had to turn towards the tree, it was dark there, the street lamps spread a blueish sheen from a distance, in the darkness the tree looked formidable, you had to go round it carefully, and there was the bank, the water was oddly viscous, and dark like all past misfortunes, so beautiful in that excitement a person gets from recovering their freedom of choice, doing what they most want, a gentle freedom of soothing and oblivion.

"You'll get your shoes wet," a man in a raincoat said sharply.

"Yes," he answered. "Yes."

"This isn't a good place," said the man. "I guess you're a foreigner."

"Yes."

"We could get a drop of something," said the man. "Let me buy you a drink."

"Do we know each other? Do you remind me of someone?"

"That I can't say," said the man in the raincoat.

"Schubert?" said Kamil.

"Who are you talking about?" asked the man. "Where's your pal?"

"I'm alone," said Kamil. "You mentioned a drink, am I right?"

"I did," said the man in the raincoat. "My treat."

"No," said Kamil. "It's on me. If I was trying to get my shoes wet, I wasn't doing it for lack of money."

"For a reason like that it's not worth getting even your little finger wet," said the man in the raincoat.

They climbed up slowly to the bridge, then walked along rather more briskly towards the Old Town; they crossed the roadway of the rue du Rhône, looked at the displays of the luxury department stores, went on to the square, past the Stork Hotel, continued up, up, it was darker there, Kamil felt his freedom of choice melting away, he was back once again in his own skin, tanned by wind, fire, and smoke, he had nothing left within him but a desire to sit down at a table with this guy, look him in the eye, and tell him that sooner or later I'll manage it anyway, don't invest in my misfortune, you'll never get anything back, do you think this is the only bridge in the world, how many bridges have I seen that you could jump off just nicely, in a magnificent, luminous arc, over meadows, over rivers, or lie down on the railroad tracks, in my time I tried an experiment like that once, it was pretty uncomfortable, that really embarrassed me, I thought that it wasn't right to set off for eternity with a sore butt, so I stood up and walked away, and five seconds later an international express train came by along those tracks, my friend, there is undoubtedly something capricious about drowning in the most elegant city in Europe, in one of the shallowest rivers, in the busiest part of the city, and before your very eyes to boot, for which I would like to apologize most sincerely, after all you'd planned to take a walk to get some exercise, and now all this unpleasant business on my account, but I didn't ask to be saved, shall we go in here, it looks quite inviting inside, let's sit down at this table, we'll have a

drink, don't ask what led me to do it, if the truth be told
you never really know, by all means, gin and tonic, I won't
make a secret of the fact that there's a woman in this, you
knew that, but to complete my confession, there are two
women involved, maybe even more, I seem to have gotten
lost in my life, too many experiences I think, too many efforts, too much pain also, something got muddled up inside me, when I say inside me, I'm referring to what
Dostoevsky used to call the soul, but the matter itself is an
ordinary one, to the extent that I feel embarrassed to talk
about it, what it is is an excess of love, which all of a sudden
I don't know what to do with, there's so much of it that the
burden can't be carried, it fills me up more and more, I'm
afraid I'll fall while crossing the street, I won't make it up
the stairs, I won't be able to lift the fork as far as my mouth,
I'm stuffed with love like the animals in a natural history
museum, like the safe in a Swiss bank, it's hard to describe,
because not everyone has experienced such a thing in life,
it's a kind of unnatural pregnancy, when the blood stops in
your veins from the excess, your lungs burst from the excess, and yet people usually complain of not having
enough, don't you think that usually it's different, people
suffer from a lack of something, we live in a civilization that
doesn't content us, doesn't satisfy our aspirations, our
desires and our longings, there's always too little of something, actually in fact it's most often love, it's very painful,
people suffer from a lack of love, but if someone wishes to
fall asleep, you understand what I mean, if someone wishes
to fall asleep in that Hamletian sense, it's only because of an
excess of it, this belief comes from my experience, which

I'd be happy to tell you about, but it won't change anything, because I can't pass my excess on to you, even if you
are empty and hungering, it's really not so complicated, the
thing is that there's a woman, high-minded, wise, beautiful,
whom I love, and who loves me too, an astounding thing,
by the way, for there's no reason why she should love
someone like me, nevertheless, my good sir, nevertheless
that's just what happened, and it would be an entirely trivial business if it weren't for the fact that there's another
woman too, who has become the bane of my existence,
there's nothing special about her, a totally ordinary person,
but at times, it's difficult for me to understand, I have a
fleeting impression, you might say it's something lyrical,
like the touch of a bird's wing in flight, or a snowflake on
one's forehead, you know what I mean, for instance the
rustle of a leaf underfoot at dusk, in the late fall, something
fleeting, and yet acute, a pain for no reason, without a
proper place, and I think it comes from the fact that I have
moments of clairvoyance, at such moments I arrive at the
conviction that these two women don't exist at all, because
I'm quite simply alone, utterly abandoned with this love of
mine, with a sackful of love on my back, I understand your
astonishment, I feel the same way myself, that's the reason
for my uncertainty, because I really can't be certain of anything any more, even my old delusions, which accompanied me for years, everything within me has undergone
some kind of change, such that things that I used to be at-
tached to fill me with disgust, things that were of no importance have become crucial, if I had a penchant for
meaningless phrases I would say I was at a crossroads, I'm

unable to decide where I should be heading, I'm running in place, that's exactly how it feels, running in place, I've already trodden out a little hollow, another week or two and my grave will be ready, I see you're not smiling, I'm grateful, one can only have talks like these with a man, we have in us a certain august quality that is never found in a woman, don't you find that even with death they take a pragmatic approach, a person is simply alive, then dies, in a woman's eyes it's a passage from one qualitative state to another, with us it's different, with us it's a lengthy process, an immensely tough task of getting used to that moment, it's accompanied by dreams and visions, a change of lifestyle, a self-examination, a search for allusions, it's really only then that we flourish internally, to put it poetically, it's only in the face of death that the butterfly is released from the cocoon of the man, but unfortunately it's too late, there's so little time left to mend anything, to begin again, differently than before, in a word there's no longer any chance of feeding the hungry, giving drink to the thirsty, consoling the afflicted, now there's only sorrow, and the feeling that so much has been wasted, but I'd like to get back to my situation, yes, I'll gladly have a brandy, a cup of coffee and a glass of brandy make it possible to hope that the world has a chance of surviving, maybe that chance still exists for me too, anyway, it's hard to express it, I just feel a big disappointment, I'm very disappointed in the Lord God, I believe in God, it's a little old-fashioned, but it ensures a degree of comfort, personal convenience, after all, what kind of a choice do we have, have you ever weighed it up? you shouldn't put it off, it's best to choose a moment of reflection, it'll allow you to reach a conclusion without that inner feverishness that sometimes overcomes us, so coming back to God, I have a choice only between Him and nothingness, in that sense He's much closer to me, I can attribute certain qualities to Him, I can create Him in my image and likeness, with nothingness you can do nothing, nothing whatsoever, and still nothing, you can't get your mind around it, whereas the Lord God, sure you can, kind of crookedly, but you can, in the belief in God there's a yearning of ours to feel warmth and care in our old age, someone will hold us, my friend, someone will wipe our tears, have you never had a feeling of terrible abandonment, all around the empty, endlessly vast world and you alone, in a street somewhere or by the sea, or in the woods, sometimes it happens without a landscape, then it's even more painful for me, I'm sitting in an attic, the attic's dark, there's just a little sunlight breaking through the cracks in the boards, down below human voices, quieter and quieter, getting farther and farther away, finally there's complete silence, I'm alone, I'm the only one left in the world, the attic and me in the attic, the door locked from the outside, not a hope of getting out, the window is boarded over, I'm sitting on some old trunk, though when I finally open it it'll turn out that it's been empty for years, so I've been left alone, even the spiders have died off, the sun has set, the night is dark, the crickets have already stopped chirping and the frogs have fallen silent in the nearby pond, I'm alone, even the wind has gone off to the other side of the earth, darkness, silence, emptiness, my poor, mortal body, which I don't need any more, it's no use for anything, there's nothing to

lift, nothing to hear, nothing to see, touch, smell, you should pay attention to the matter of the senses, it's they that torment us most, because it's through them that we perceive the world, but losing them is precisely nothing-ness, it's the senses that suggested a metaphysical solution to me, because if God exists, they become necessary once more in order for me to be able to listen to God and watch Him, touch His robe and feel upon myself the wind of His eternal nature, hence my conviction about people's need for God, it's probably a form of cowardice, dodging the ra-tional conception of our dignity that ought to distinguish us as higher creatures, more intellectually developed, yet at certain moments, in an hour of great despair a person throws their intellect on the scrapheap, their dignity too, and simply weeps from fear and loneliness, and when that person raises their eyes, through their tears they try to make out the image of God from their childhood, and at just that moment God comes to them, hence those last-minute conversions, which are not motivated by fear but by an immense longing, those conversions arise, I believe, from our need for freedom, for if we have only nothingness before us, there's nothing in that nothingness, including no freedom, so how else can freedom be saved but by choos-ing to believe in God, who is also freedom, or perhaps only He is freedom, don't you think, all this is awfully difficult for me, I'm slipping, falling downwards, in the mist and darkness of my pain, yet there is also something uncom-monly strong in my heart, some immense power, for if you think it was your appearance today that cooled my desire for a dip in the Rhône, you're guilty of the sin of pride, imagine if you will that at that moment, which might even have been my last, I suddenly felt something that held me back, and it was the arms of that woman, she took me in her arms, I smelled the fragrance of her hair, I saw her eyes, my friend, they are eyes like the sailboats of Christ's fishermen from two thousand years ago, to tell the truth it's actually in her eyes that I sometimes discern a tiny yet quite clear outline, and that is His presence . . .

And now I'd like to be alone. I'm tired, my life would like to fall asleep, my friend . . .

For a long, long time he sat on the bench in the shade of the tree, listening intently to the murmur of the water, the hum of the city over his head, and also to his own voices, at first clamorous, angry, rebellious, howling, then dropping gradually to the kind of whisper in which one recites a prayer of humility and reconciliation.

In the end he stood up from the bench, for he finally felt strengthened. He glanced at the frothing current of water and it suddenly seemed alien to him, distant somehow, like a fire that had once burned him, like rubble that had once buried him, like worlds in which he had once disappeared without a trace. With a slow, rather weary step he crossed the metal footbridge to the embankment.

It occurred to him that it would be a nice idea to have a drink.

Ruth, he thought, I'll have a glass of brandy and I'll go back to you. I have no world other than the one you hold tight in the palm of your small hand, whenever I have a wish to kiss it.